PORTABLE PEOPLE

by

Paul West

Drawings by Joe Servello

Books by Paul West

Fiction
Lord Byron's Doctor
The Place in Flowers Where Pollen Rests
Rat Man of Paris
The Very Rich Hours of Count von Stauffenberg
Gala
Colonel Mint
Caliban's Filibuster
Bela Lugosi's White Christmas
I'm Expecting to Live Quite Soon
Alley Jaggers
Tenement of Clay
The Universe, and Other Fictions

Nonfiction
Portable People
Sheer Fiction
Out of My Depths
Words for a Deaf Daughter
The Wine of Absurdity
I, Said the Sparrow
The Snow Leopard
Byron and the Spoiler's Art

This book is for Sam Vaughan of course.

Some of these sketches have appeared in different form in: *Air and Space, City Lights Review, Conjunctions, Harper's, The Nation, New American Review, The New York Times, The Paris Review, Parnassus, Review, TriQuarterly,* and *The Washington Post.*

Library of Congress Cataloging-in-Publication Data

West, Paul, 1930–
    Portable people / Paul West.
       p.   cm.
    ISBN 0-945167-35-0
    I. Title.
PR6073.E766P67   1990
813'.54—dc20

                           90-1691
                           CIP

ACKNOWLEDGMENTS

This book could not have been put together without the help and ingenuity of the following people, to whom I express my gratitude: Diane Ackerman, Burt Britton, Bill and Sheila Forster, Karel Husa, Charles Mann, Carl Sagan, Joe and Lisa Schall, Alicia Schonbrun, Sandra Steltz, Rolf Stundt, Mildred West, and of course Joe Servello, not only the drawer of these faces but also an inspired researcher in his own right. I am also indebted to the following for encouragement and ideas: Susan Bell, Herbert Leibowitz, David Madden of Sacramento, Elaine Markson, Bradford Morrow, and George Plimpton. Sam Vaughan suggested adding photographs and so became the book's instigating visionary.

CONTENTS

SAMUEL PEPYS

Pepys's *Diary,* one-and-a-quarter-million words concerning nine-and-a-half years of agitated but not always scrutinized living, is bound to disappoint the moralist. At least, it must disappoint the intelligent moralist who, whether reading or writing, likes to delve into motives, dilemmas, and justifications. For Pepys conspicuously omits excuses: child of a libertine age, he races into his fornications and carousals with no more sense of self-control than a lemming. He manages at the same time to do his job extremely well. This Commissioner of the Navy, Clerk of the Acts, and Treasurer of the Tangier Commission is too intelligent to be a slovenly administrator, too anxious to increase his "crumb" to risk adding incompetency to the dangers of keeping well in with a capricious regime. As he scrambles his ignominious, or struts his official, way among the ropedancers, drolls, music booths, shipyard carpenters, whores, gallants, book-shops, taverns, and theaters of London at its most corrupt and most noisome, he caters blindly to his twin drives: pelf (by which to secure the estate of his dreams) and sex. Not that he was a miser or a victim of inexorable satyriasis; he could be both generous and continent, even a lavish spender and an ascetic. But he liked to keep exact accounts and, after an early spell of tentativeness, to spice his sexual life with variety. No frequenter of brothels, he was a diffident tickler of enthusiastic amateurs—usually servants or scheming wives. His true Penelope was Barbara, the Lady Castlemaine, unattainable and in some ways uncannily like his own wife, Elizabeth.

But no ideal wrecked him, unless his almost realized one of a perpetually complaisant or unwitting Elizabeth. After years of assiduous womanizing, he had to undergo the first long bout of her fury; oddly enough, the discovery that her stodgy, watery-eyed husband was a lecher stimulated her into being, for the first time in her devoted and incompetent life, anxious to get Samuel into bed. Pepys, musing on the shifts and pranks of fortune, took his medicine. Occasionally he had played little games of self-denial with himself: forswearing women for theaters and drink—on moral grounds; then renouncing the last two for the first—because venery was cheaper. He was as capable of pious self-accusation as of shock at the misdemeanors of friends. Perhaps the responsibilities of office developed his carnal side extraordinarily, so that his private life became a caper. Certainly, seeing him as we do in the *Diary,* bit after bit, we cannot help noting his gift for making the grotesque abound.

To punish his wife he pulls her nose; having blacked her eye (when the nose seemed an insufficient target) he treats her with endearments, butter and parsley; when she goes out in drawers rather than in a shift, he assumes her intentions chaste.

4

She, piqued, reads him Sir Philip Sidney on jealousy; most of the time she devours French popular romances. He eclectically plods through Fuller's *Church History of England* and extols the information value of Helot's pornographic *L'Escolle des Filles*. He reads Ovid aloud to her; she, in the room above his study, takes dancing lessons from a suave *maître*. Rushing home one day, he flies upstairs only to surprise Lady Sandwich "doing something upon the pott" in the dining room. In the evenings he has the maid comb his hair, fondling her front as she does it; he plugs the flageolet into his heavy-featured, covetous face; or he slinks off to a cabaret with a drab. Back at the office next day, he imposes fines upon himself; each kiss, after the first, to cost him twelvepence for the poor. He suffers from colic, his wife from dysmenorrhea. A born survivor, he evades the pox, gets himself and his periwig regularly denitted, comes through the plague and then runs headlong into the Committee on Miscarriages. A navy matter, this; he has been paying seamen by ticket. But, fortified with sack and a brandy, he speaks brilliantly in the Commons for almost four hours. Even the king congratulates him. He is the Cicero of the navy. But, when Buckingham succeeds Clarendon, Pepys's patrons are ousted from power. Yet he survives to survive Whig plots, but not the stone, of which he dies in 1703.

The Pepys, who signed himself Dapper Dickey when writing notes to Mary Knep, seems adept at inspissation—at thickening up his life until it has the quality of something magnified: a tegument with a defiant bristle in every pore.

5

CAROLUS LINNAEUS

As a boy, Linnaeus often played truant from school to roam the countryside looking for plants; and he enjoyed playing doctor to his brothers and sisters, making a lancet out of wood and pretending to bleed them. The two habits belonged together on a more serious, worldly plane too, as, at that time, doctors had to be botanists as well. Not long after, he was classifying the plants of a particular local district and journeying to Stockholm to attend the dissection of a woman whose hanging had been postponed to a moment convenient for the College of Medicine. Note how the naturalist and the clinician play into each other's hands, each prosaically feeding Linnaeus the lyric poet who prefaced his *Lapland Journey* with a little, unpunctuated prose poem ("*Clouds* have I passed through," he wrote, "The *World's End* have I visited").

The rest of his life was really a prolongation of this journey and the habits of scrupulous observation developed during it. Wherever he went, Linnaeus spotted or learned unusual things and wrote them down. Lapps wore birch-bark collars; strained milk through plaited hair from cows' tails; had magic drums, which the local missionaries demanded they surrender or be bled in the main artery of the arm. Gelded reindeer is fatter than nongelded and so of great value to the Lapps, whose highest term of praise is "a castrated reindeer." He describes in detail the pudendum of an ancient Lapp and learns how to cure chilblains with toasted reindeer cheese and how to make thread from the tendons of reindeer hooves.

Going farther afield, he debunks the famous seven-headed Hydra of Hamburg (concocted from weasels and snake skins) and in England gets a hothouse banana tree to flower while speculating about its being the forbidden tree in Eden. He invents the so-called Celsius thermometer and soon becomes famous for his "sexual" classification based on stamens and pistils. In passing, he makes ironical notes on the rakes of Stockholm and soon begins treating them by the score with mercury. He impresses the royal court with gum tragacanth lozenges and even inspects such relics of Scandinavian witchcraft as eagles' claws for colic. In 1744, writing in the semi-hagiographical third person, he discovers he is a happy man ("Fame, the work for which he had been born, enough money . . . a beloved wife, handsome children, and an honored name"). Like his French contemporary, Buffon, he goes on classifying but finds time to ponder the oddly constructed sexual organs of the raccoon and deliver semiformal lectures on diet ("Mutton is best for sedentary workers . . . pork for manual workers"). He saves his newborn daughter's life with the kiss of life on one day and on another seems to anticipate Priestley's discovery of oxygen ("The air we inhale has electricity, the air we exhale has not"). Coffee he denounces. Gout he cures with wild strawberries. And, in a bizarre tract called *Nemesis Divina,* he spells out to his libidinous only son the facts of incest, adultery, and masturbation, even explaining how wives punish their mates by making coition unpleasant in a hundred different ways.

At fifty-one he is morose in the extreme ("Had I a rope and English courage I would long since have hanged myself. I fear that my wife is again pregnant"), but he is soon breeding artificial pearls with globules of plaster of Paris introduced into mussels. His mind treks on, slowed by sciatica and angina. In constant pain that only draughts of beer drained in a single gulp can ease, he dies on the tenth of January 1778, having left instructions to "entertain nobody at my funeral, and accept no condolences." Six years later, by a quirk of history, his libraries and collections accompany Sir James Edward Smith to England and now rest in London's Burlington House.

The man who emerges is earthy, vain, cantankerous, but preternaturally alert; a titan to experts but, to the ordinary reader, an untapped source of captivating eyeball witness, an off-duty commentator somewhere between Li Po and Thomas Gray. Here he is, for instance, on the landscape of Skane: "RED as blood are often whole slopes of *Viscaria.* WHITE as snow are sandfields of the sweet-smelling *Dianthus.* DAP-

PLED are the waysides with *Echium, Cichorium, Anchusa* and *Malva."* Here is a page from his *Calendar of Flora:*

Dec.	xxii.	Butter shrinks and separates from the sides of the tub.
	xxiii.	Alp flower buds begin to open.
Jan.	i.	Ice on lakes begins to crack.
	ii.	Wooden walls snap in the night. Cold frequently extreme at this time, the greatest observed was 55.7.
	iv.	Horse dung spurts.
	viii.	Epiphany rains.
	xxvi.	St. Paul's rains.
Feb.	xxii.	Very cold nights often between Feb. 20 and 28, called STEEL NIGHTS.

And here, his view of death and regeneration, is a bit of quite unmelancholy post-Hamlet meditation:

The fairest maid's cheeks can become the ugliest henbane, and the arm of the most stalwart Hercules the frailest pondweed. This is eaten by a stinking cimex (bedbug) and becomes such an animal. This cimex is then eaten by birds and becomes a bird; the bird is eaten by man and thus becomes a part of him.

JOHN CLARE WALKING
TO THE HORIZON

Only that line is level. Only that line is Godlike enough to withdraw from me as I gain on it. Only that line is infinitely mine, as unseeable apart from its earth as the outline of a strawberry from its fruit. Only that line curves and comes leaning round behind me, lest I go lummocking back like a homesick pigeon. Only that line invites and snubs. I dote on it, wanting to inhale its fishing-line length, chomp down on the wide slice of its grin. It has no language, it has no place to live; but I am certain that, if I walk and run, run and walk, keeping it for ever in view like those lines they rig around the globe, one of these all-alike days I will tread over it and, untripped, walk clean into the mind of God, all set out like a sensible vegetable garden whose sundial is piled high with carrots. *Enter, John,* I'll hear. *Come see what your eyes were on.*

JOHN KEATS

He is the perfect image of the compulsive maker who, burning away with a sickness he could not defeat, exploited it for his own purposes. Increasingly consumed, he consumed life itself; "Nothing seemed to escape him," wrote his friend Joseph Severn, not even "the features and gestures of passing tramps, the colour of one woman's hair, the smile on one child's face." He entered into everything, his intensity was homogeneous, yet his morbidity wasn't always solemn, his singlemindedness wasn't monomania. He wasn't a Cockney for nothing; beleaguered and harassed, he anticipated the bombed Cockneys of the blitz who, dicing nightly with death, conducted business as usual in the daylight. Trouble came home to roost, so—although grumbling and given to savage despondency—he studied it on its perch; studied it to death. That apprenticeship, through which Keats eventually gained the by no means negligible qualification of Licentiate of the Society of Apothecaries, stabilized him: but in an avocation only. Poetry had to come first, a vocation as uncertain and traumatic as his childhood had been (at eight-and-a-half he lost his father; two months later Mrs. Keats remarried; then all four children went to live with their maternal grandmother; all this in just over a year). School understandably became his haven, poetry his compensation, women his confusion (he always distinguished between good women and those who were sexually attractive).

We see him slipping live minnows into his grandmother's wash-tub; declining to waltz, the female waistlines of the time being awkwardly high for one so stocky; "Nectarine sucking—and Melon carving" with his small sister; striking a schoolmaster at age thirteen; noting down curiosa from anatomy lectures; puzzling for a consistent view of Byron, Wordsworth, and Hazlitt respectively; sporting a false mustache; entering into fifteen-minute sonnet competitions with Leigh Hunt; bathing in the Isis during an Oxford heat-wave; dosing himself with mercury and laudanum; wincing at *The Chieftain's Daughter*, Covent Garden's oriental equivalent of a modern Western; drinking claret and trading giggled obscenities with two parsons; disagreeing with Wordsworth only to have Mrs. Wordsworth rebuke him with "Mr. Wordsworth is never interrupted"; imitating the sounds of bassoon and flageolet; coining "bitcherell" to partner doggerel; likening himself to Hamlet; acquiring in Scotland a taste for whisky; sleeping the night on the earth floor of a shepherd's cottage; climbing Ben Nevis; feeling something of himself die at the deathbed of his brother Tom; spectating at a barefisted thirty-four-round-boxing match; getting his eye blacked by a cricket ball; coughing up a spot of blood he at once recognizes as arterial; receiving Fanny Brawne's last gift, a cornelian stone used for cooling the hands while doing needlework; fretting or joking during the miserable, preposterous sea journey to Italy; emptying a bad *trattoria* meal out of the window; hemorrhaging five times in nine days; fondling to the last that white cornelian as if, according to Severn, it were "the only thing left him in this world clearly tangible." After a life of grievous, productive hurry, he was dead at twenty-five years and four months, an age at which many poets have not even started.

JOHN WILLIAM
POLIDORI

Lord Byron's doctor and traveling companion, John Polidori, was dead by his own hand at twenty-six, having taken a potion he himself had brewed, based on prussic acid; but then, all through his time in Europe as part of Byron's entourage, he had been trying out one form of suicide or another. He was a man perpetually on the edge, almost a *maudit,* and his manner—alternating between sulks and effusive silliness—early on began to provoke Byron beyond endurance (he several times thought of killing him off, either by drowning or in a duel).

Polidori was a prodigy, the youngest man ever to receive a medical degree from Edinburgh University, and he came from an artistic family: his father had translated *The Castle of Otranto* into Italian, and he was the uncle of the future Dante Gabriel and Christina Rossetti.

At first he amused Byron and had so earned the honor of traveling as a near equal with the most famous man in England. He had also been promised 500 guineas by Byron's publisher,

John Murray, for a full diary of Byron's doings while abroad. Polidori kept that diary but was dissuaded from publishing it. After his death, his aging sister ripped out of it what she thought the obscenest pages and allowed it into the world (it came out in 1911), but it is clear from what such initiates as William Michael Rossetti said that Polidori had set down every instance he had witnessed of Byron's sex life (Rossetti remembered a chambermaid raped in Ostend, for instance).

It is odd to think of a doctor in such a constant ferment of emotion, as full of malice and masochism as Polidori was, always bringing to the fore Byron's latent sadism. He used Polidori as a butt and Polidori seethed. He ridiculed his amours, his verse, his ideas, and even gossiped that something unholy was going on in Polidori's medical career: all his patients died, and he seemed more interested in dissection than in prophylaxis or cure. At one point, perhaps to get away from a medical scandal threatening in Italy, Polidori planned to go to Brazil, to make a fresh start on fresh meat, as Byron quipped, and it was clearly dangerous to entrust one's body to his flighty, devious hands.

An image builds of a man who, despite his levity and charm, was too highly strung for his own good: a plagiarist, a hanger-on, a climber, a satanist who was also a klutz and a social menace. The novelist Stendhal watched him getting arrested at the Milan Opera and left a long, detailed account of it, and Byron's table-talk leaves one in no doubt as to the bickering that went on between the two of them. Eventually Byron had to let him go and paid him off. Polidori became a gambler and took his own life in August 1821, upon which event Byron commented, "Poor Polly is gone."

THOMAS CARLYLE'S MOTHER

How could only the one hand be moving and all the rest of him be still as the Cairngorms? His mind they say is like a cottage on the move, as if it had wheels. They say his eyes blaze forth. I say his hands do at least when he writes to me. Fancy learning to read just so you can read your bairn's letters. Or I did it to keep snoopers from getting between him and me. Those who read letters for you because you are one of the world's helpless, daft as a gull. Soon, Mother, he says, you will be reading about the French and the Germans I write about. He says he goes off the deep end so often in his books the London folk call him the Diver. To me he's a loch anyway. I can read his hand. He can read my hands or he could if they weren't all cracked from suds and chapped with wind. He spells chilblain for me and I am going to ask him what a *blain* is because it has a good Scots sound to it. The trouble is that anybody who can write with such an open hand to his mother might open his hand to the wrong other woman and then no amount of book writing can save him. There were better words between us when I could read no better than a haggis. If only he might find the right lass that was so fond of him she gave up language altogether and letter writing and letter reading. She would care that much and never read his to me or mine to him. Your loving I sign myself and then say who I am.

EMILY BRONTË

Brontë! as well as recalling the Greek for thunder, the word evokes Jurassic giants at play on the Yorkshire moors. People of that region speak of Brontës as of a genus of awesome, obsolete beings maybe still invigilating what goes on. Thanks to the local cult, there are Brontë gewgaws, but Bontëan also means brooding, primal, stormy, something ferally mysterious, as if the head of the Medusa itself were made of Yorkshire pudding, or as if Branwell's dipsomaniac and narcotic excesses had fused with Emily's attunement to the ineffable and the slow, pictorial swell of Charlotte's gothic horror. (Anne, the least dynamic of the frail sisters, tends to get left out, but her part in the fabrication of the Gondal fantasies cannot be ignored, nor her role as Emily's lifelong confidante.) Clearly, if the Brontës had not existed, someone would have been obliged to invent them. They personify a dionysian yet half-puritan intensity that matches the bleak moorland landscape and sends us afield to the compulsive lugubriousness of Bartók's Bluebeard and the spaced-out fulminations of King Lear on the heath. Theirs is the poetry of overcast, the agon of the damp.

I says theirs, but what has come be regarded as Brontëan is mostly Emily, an amazing fact on the strength of *Wuthering Heights* and a handful of relentlessly explanatory, rather ordinary poems. Charlotte (who seems more tedious the more we learn about her) outlived them all, but she was too stable to be a visionary and her novels lack the sulfuric élan which was Emily's own, not filched from Byron or Sir Walter Scott or *Blackwood's Magazine. Wuthering Heights,* in fact, reads like a dance before death, an orchestration of Emily's ambivalent feeling that, on the one hand, her life was an interruption of some preferable state, and, on the other, that (as Catherine Earnshaw puts it) "heaven did not seem to be my real home." It is the worst of the abiding human dilemmas and it has brought a powerful lot of literature into being, all of it palpable shadowboxing, all the way from Boethius to Beckett, in whose company Emily Brontë belongs.

Winifred Gérin, who biographized all the Brontës except the father and lived for ten years at Haworth poring over Brontë materials preserved at the parsonage, makes an excellent point concerning Emily's last months. "It is her conduct during that period, known to readers of Charlotte's letters and of Mrs. Gaskell's *Life,* that has been allowed to characterize her whole existence, though in truth it was highly uncharacteristic of her." Emily's aloofness and intractability during that time seem appropriate for someone who lost her faith in death and paradoxically, therefore, also lost the will to live. It is resolute lethargy adapted into a technique, much as she adapted death, the source of her disappointment, into an instrument with which to abolish *ennui*. Clearly she was too far gone to recoil into life again along the lines of the affirmation written in 1841:

> . . . *Few hearts to mortals given*
> *On Earth so wildly pine;*
> *Yet none would ask a Heaven*
> *More like this Earth than thine* .

Anne was dying, too, and the prospect of life without her amounted, as Gérin says, to "another unspeakable menace that Emily had to face." The Emily of the last months is an appallingly moving figure, not so much out of character, I think, as brought full circle and then farther, past even her starting point, and trapped with none of her lifetime's beliefs to sustain her. She is as dumbfounded as Beckett's Unnamable. She could not see Branwell live, or then die, without calling into question the whole purpose of life. Medically speaking, she died of an illness brought on by a cold caught at Branwell's funeral service, and only three months later; but the virus had a metaphysical impact, too.

A girl of singular reticence, she was never studious. Housework (of which she did a lot) she never chafed at, for her mind was always on something else. In spite of the presence of Branwell and her father, she was a *Hausfrau* without a

Herr. She wrote a more than passable French, a superb English, prose, but the act of publication—like Branwell's drunken confessions—inspired only disgust in her. Yet she sent out *Wuthering Heights* to successive firms despite repeated rejections and devoted herself to Branwell like some saintly practical nurse. Ferociously self-critical, she haughtily sided with failures and dogs, in church sat with her back to the pulpit, in the village ignored everybody. When she was certain she was almost dead, she finally agreed to see a doctor. The only one of the Brontë children not to undergo a religious crisis in adolescence, she spent much of her time on *thou* terms with a Supreme Being she never once called the Absolute. A mystic, she had none of the childhood revelations spoken of by such other mystics as Traherne, Vaughan, and Wordsworth. Her intense interior life began late and left her early, and she ended up in the cruel position of a fan who had a sustained long-distance call from a deity who in the end hung up on her, leaving her hung up on him. She left not faith but of that was left. Wherever you look, the contradictions pile up and you have only her sturdy, coiling prose to hold on to.

Understand her? It's difficult, not least because Charlotte destroyed manuscripts that *might* have told us much; the second novel, advanced enough for Emily to approach a publisher about it, vanished too. Instead, while never forgetting "the hidden ghost which has its home in me" (or had until the last few months), we can unforgettably see her, like some nympholeptic peasant Georges Bernanos might have invented, drawing a pert portrait of the north wind; stooping her tall body over the bread she made and baked with such expertness; domesticating a merlin hawk, and installing tame geese in the house along with her pet mastiff; turning the young princess Victoria into a Gondal heroine; sleeping on the camp bed or, clad in a shawl, writing in her unheated bedroom (not even a fireplace); quelling combatant dogs with pepper and her bare fists or, after being bitten, cauterizing the wound with a hot smoothing iron; out pistol-shooting with her father; buying shares in the York and North Midland Railway; serving as fire-brigade when Branwell set fire to his bed; on the day before she died carrying an apronful of broken meat and bread for the dogs and being almost upended by a gust of wind. Her coffin was the narrowest the village carpenter had ever made for an adult: only sixteen inches across.

Her curbed life is vivid, and to us, as to her, it makes no sense; when teleology finally broke down, leaving her with a nature full of the unnecessary, empty of its opposite, she found herself in a predicament, familiar to all of us, in which the body is merely a bicycle for the redundant mind to ride.

CAPTAIN AHAB:
A Novel by
the White Whale

I too, alone, survived to tell thee. A whale tells this, white as Biscay froth, a tale black as caviar. I almost lost heart. Albinos do, doomed special while feeling like the rest. We're dark unto ourselves. *We?* I am the only one. I have never bred. I have never seen a white male or a white mate. I never had company save for him. Only, during brief heaven, a mother who nudged and nourished. Shunned, I go from ocean to ocean, falling in love with icebergs and fluffy fog, and, nearer shore, with snow and polar bears. I am forbidden nothing, but there is nothing I can have. What sex am I? Did Ahab know?

Squinting aft, I see him, rib cage and all. As the years went by, he began to rattle, then to chime. I read his last will and testament from his lips, then took him down for the count, poor piscuniak of a mariner. Then I whale-hummed at him, just to be friendly. I wanted somehow to swing him loose, then pop him down, minnow-small and feather-frail. Install him on the bulby mound of one vast kidney according to Jonah Law. A pet, a familiar, a love.

But dislodge him I could not, and I soon knew his coming for what it was: a test in the form of a sign, a sign in the form of a test. Could I brook his presence without wanting friendship? Ahab was my birthmark. Yes. "Ishmael, art thou sleeping there below?" Then answer would come: "Moby, I am thine, forever."

It was all hopeless. Call me, I began, but my still-thundering jelly of a heart floated upward through my mouth, jump-a-thump, and all that's left is an infolded compass rose, miming its thanks, murmuring a dew.

NICOLÒ PAGANINI

Eyes like red-hot coals; face attenuated and gruesomely concave; my lips, two mating earthworms: the clichés of my diabolical appearance have still not died away. I must have been intolerably vivid.

Nor have the rumors gone, either. The G-string of my Guarnerius was supposed to have been cut from the intestines of a murdered mistress. I was obliged to publish my mother's letters just to prove I had human sire and dam. And while my cadaver reposed in its coffin, first in Nice, and then at Villefranche, it supposedly emitted the sounds of a violin. Has the great world not yet wearied of such tarradiddle? I fear Paganini still fares forth aboard the *Flying Dutchman,* as of old.

Yet, death be praised, there are no more Grillparzers to versify in my honor. No more Paganini gloves, Paganini bread-rolls, Paganini pretzels. The day of the "Paganini coup" at billiards—an impossibly screwed ball that caromed away its unholy energy—has gone. No one is saying, "Paganini is a solitary man in his art" or "He is because he *is* and not because others *were*, before him." Amen to all et cetera.

I told Rossini, "Gioacchino, I am neither young nor handsome. I am very ugly. But when women hear my voice, my melting tones, they begin weeping, and then I become their idol, and they lie at my feet." It was all too easy.

In Leghorn once, a string snapped. The canaille sniggered. But on I played, right through an intricate passage, like some virtuoso Theseus. With three strings instead of four. Often enough, after that, I started out with worn strings, just in hopes of a skill-taxing mishap. Oh yes, I was a fake of a sort.

So much for trivia. So much for triumph. Cancer, however, does not yield so readily to improvisation, to ocean voyages, or even to fame. As I came to grips with its tightening hold on me, in Nice, I coughed, oh, such a Paganini cough, and by 1838 had altogether lost my voice.

Able to improvise dementedly on the violin, I awaited my end, my ears full of bubbling or buzzing jelly, my brain trapped as ever between scatology and hell: I, Niccolò, the Machiavelli of catgut, *diminuendo*.

And then I saw it: I still had prospects. After death. I dreamed an electric cry across my broken vocal cords; whatever your caprice, or your aversion to the nacreous, black, holy froth that coats them, give a helping hand. Bring your fingers near them, then pluck and play.

JACK THE RIPPER

We were three. Roaming the night. In our stagecoach. Netley, he drove. Sickert charmed them, Sickert the painter, charmed the whores, up to us, from the streets. I lulled them, one by one, to easy death, with poisoned grapes, then opened them, sliced with knives, I, William Gull, the Crown's physician. We three frightened, we ordinary three, a whole century. To oblige Victoria, whose helpless grandson, little Prince Eddy, married a slut. In sordid secret. Four women knew. Four women died. At our hands. I lopped innards. To a clip-clop. A bloody trinity. We were that. Serving the queen. The blackmail coach. The Ripper team. Sent our letter. To the press. Address: "from Hell." No, another place. Then we stopped. Grapes, knives, coach. All three gone. All three men. All four women. No one caught. Much too clever. To be famous. London loved us.

FEODOR CHALIAPIN

My voice was such a Volga orgy, lardies unt gentleschnitches, zat, ven I sprang a title role, no longer ze burly peasant I once was, but *really Boris,* I could turn toward the wings and without breaking cadence or tone command my offstage servant "Go-oo to-oo thee Haut Elle art vance and breeng me the Vine Ay Four Gott." *Da.* They were listening to my face, much as, later, they worshiped at Stalin's mustache. On waxen cylinders I still rise from the mud like an Egyptian pharaoh, *basso profundo del tutto mondo.* Yet where is my Chaliapinograd? Whose is my voice now?

AUGUSTE RODIN

God's dong, if such a thing can be, is a velvet hammer made of love that thumps the stars home, where they belong, in the moist pleat of the empyrean. Surely he needs no goading on, unlike myself, finger-dipping each and every cleft of every model, and all that a mere preliminary to what goes on after the day's work is done, and we twist the big key clockwise. That is when I get my girls to tongue one another before my very eyes. It is almost as if the sculpting is mere prelude to the venery. By midnight, they are all going their ways, about their business, with Rodin syrup dribbling from them as they walk, like molten marble. Those who pose for me must taste my will, upended like ducks on a pond.

When my Balzac, now, strides forth with upright phallus in his fist, from behind he must be read as a giant lingam marching to India. I mean these burly semblances to stun, my lord, as when, for Becque and sundry appreciative madams, I turn actor and behead with a sword the plaster statues arranged in front of me. Those who cry out, in abuse, "Rodin is a great big prick" are right. I am always and ever the policeman's son, neither peasant nor poet.

I receive on Sundays, as my copy of *The Guide to the Pleasures of Paris* says, married to that carthorse, Rose, who gave me a son with a broken brain; abandoned by Camille, who once adored me and now in the asylum murmurs, "So this is what I get for all I did." At least she, unlike my Yankee heiress Claire, fat and daubed and drunk, never kept leaving the dinner table to go and throw up, as now, or play her creaky gramophone while my public sits around me, hearing me tell them yet again that it was indeed I who stove in Isadora Duncan, pommeling that little earlike hole between her lively legs, and it was also I who, like the milkman delivering, brought her weekly orgasm to little sad Gwen John in her rented room. I snapped her like a wineglass stem but made her coo all the same.

When I get Upstairs, His Nibs and I are going to go on such a masterful rampage the angels will cry to be raped, neuter as they are, and none shall contain us, we shall be so massive in our roistering, from the hand-gallop to the common swyve, with our humpbacked fists banged deep into the soft clay of eternity.

MAURICE MAETERLINCK

In 1906 Gide sat in Maeterlinck's box at the Mathurins Theatre where Georgette Leblanc, Maeterlinck's mistress, was playing in *La Mort de Tintagiles*. Gide later noted in his journal: "Complete uninterestedness on Maeterlinck's face; materialism of his features; a man of the North, very positive, very practical, with whom mysticism is a mode of psychic exoticism." That rebuke about mysticism is a little smug: Gide, to whom it applies also, is dissimulating. But in his own limitedly shrewd way he has spotted the ambivalence—the dour man with the rapturous inner life—that makes Maeterlinck hard to label.

There were two Maeterlincks, each living from 1862 to 1949; but the moralist who first appeared in *Le Trésor des humbles* (1896)—"very positive, very practical"—took a long time to get over two simultaneous infatuations, each of which kept urging him into the theater. One was Georgette, for whom he created his *femmes forte:* Monna Vanna the sensuous, Joyzelle the beauty, Tatiana the mixture of evil and self-denial, Marie-Victoire the flower of connubial bliss, and Marie-Magdeleine the courtesan who learns the inevitability of self-sacrifice. These are the queens of significant silences. They all face Destiny gamely. When pushed to the edge of the macrocosm they fend off Death with Phèdre-like intensity and banal language. That is the nearest they come to finding the blue bird, the symbol of cosmic happiness; and even the children in that forbiddingly anagogic elaboration of Barrie, *L'Oiseau bleu,* fail to track it down.

Being also infatuated with symbolism, Maeterlinck preferred the unknown to truth. The plays baffle and annoy. Their meaty ethical problems disappear into portentous obscurity—dark deeds into a black of nuance. Steady anaphora builds up the tension, but suddenly all dissolves into whimsy. (The only way to convey mystical experience in plays is, as Eliot has shown, to pretend to make it look ordinary.) In 1910, however, at the apogee of his dramatic career, with the Nobel prize in the offing, Maeterlinck begins an essay that develops into one of his most important books: *La Mort.* This brooding treatise begins his mature exploration of life's precariousness; the inscrutable macrocosm has given way to a microcosm of bees, "the intelligence of flowers," termites, and ants. In 1911 he meets Renée Dahon, whom he will eventually marry. From now on his best goes into his essays; he even confesses to writing out of sheer habit. The "Northerner" streak in him prompts a dozen collections of essays and three books of "popular science." The naturalist and bestiarist supplant the lover of faery; and a further dozen

plays, all feeble, cannot disguise his affinity with, say, Camus
rather than with Villiers de l'Isle Adam. He moves from the
Senecan to the Pascalian, from the gimmicky to a bare *que
sais-je?*

Personally, I find the post-Nobel Maeterlinck, his mind freed
of cults, fascinating; I wish we knew more about Maeterlinck's
motorcycle, boxing, tone deafness, roller skating, submachine
gun, two wristwatches, admiration for Salazar, quarrel with
Debussy, and misadventures in an adoring America. Here was
a man whose *summa* was no system. He persistently quoted
Marcus Aurelius's "Nothing can fall out of the universe"; his
quest for a "mystic morality" yielded to "total agnosticism;"
in *Le Grand Secret* (1921), a history of occult and esoteric
doctrines, he is the perfect heir of Pico della Mirandola. *Les
Justiciers,* written in America probably as a film scenario, sends
one at once to Camus's *juge-pénitent,* for Maeterlinck's Salomon
(a judge) redeems himself by saving the life of a little boy.
The thesis of *La Grande Loi* (1933) is "the law of universal
attraction on which are grafted the Einsteinian phantoms of
relativity." Perhaps this medley of agnosticism, science, panthe-
ism, stoicism, Renaissance syncretism, and amateur entomology
yielded few practical results. Yet, for anyone who enjoys the
spectacle of a robust-minded man publishing his confusions as
they arise, it is enthralling. If he had not been so fond of the
unknown he would have found confusion less enlightening and
pessimism less exotic.

51

MARIE CURIE

Before she became famous, she lived on bread, butter, and tea, so presumably she would have fallen asleep easily but for the caffeine. She comes alive again and again on the *Late Late Show,* thanks to the amphibious self-assurance of Greer Garson, who has the haughtiest, fruitiest voice in film history. Marie and her Pierre crouch and peer into the other room, where something glows relentlessly, a mere smudge in a shallow crucible: a dose of light. In an old shed that nobody else wanted, they render pitchblende down until they have enough. The roof leaks, their hands burn. Pierre goes out and buys some jewelry for a very beautiful woman and never returns, run down by a dray. Uranium outlives and outstrips them both; radium, too, of which President Warren G. Harding gives her one gram, paid for by American women. It is almost as much as the Institut de Radium itself has in stock, in Paris. They handle radioactive material as if it were smoked salmon. She names polonium after her native Poland. I am always going to have to wonder to whose sanctity I am responding—Curie's or Garson's, Marie's or Mrs. Miniver's—when the smudge in the other room glows again and the piano and the E-flat clarinet do what they do in Samuel Barber's version of Saint-Exupéry's *Night Flight:* pinging madly when the pilot gets off course. That featherweight belfry chimes in my ears from my fourteenth year and has almost become the signature tune of those who discover what makes the world go round, like Louis Pasteur, or design a masterpiece like Galileo's pendulum in no time at all. Ever a boy worshipper at the shrine of those who find things out on spinning celluloid, I sometimes wonder if radium, pasteurization, the magic bullet, double helixes and single, all those chinks in mother nature's blowsy armor, come into being not so much for our good in crude physical terms as for our delectation, so that we can savor the goodness and the breath-held holiness of the heart's emotions in the context of something *non pareil* that has no emotions at all, no human face, but brings home to us in many pinpoints of absolute light God's reticent impertinence, without which who would even dream of blasphemy? To us the universe is an enormous toy, and I am willing to put up with any amount of Greer Garson's hoity-toity hokum to have it brought to me on the level of a junior-grade chemistry set whose compact wonders leave me in a fearful, infatuated silence as I wonder if the eerie peace brought on by beta blockers may not be *the* peace that passes understanding. Thanks to B-movies and their oh-so-human art of watered-down epiphany.

THE WRIGHT BROTHERS

Reading about them and their advances is sometimes more moving than comedy or tragedy. There is a mode of apprehension in between (call it apprehensiveness or gifted nervousness) that amounts to common sense made eloquent, as when they decided to experiment with the cross-sections of wings and, first, flew them around on bicycle wheels then at a far from constant speed took them billowing and wafting while they, Orville and Wilbur, rode the bicycles themselves.

The homemade miracle arrives when they choose to move the air instead of the wing and call the resulting enclosure a *wind tunnel*. I exult when I think of what they hit on next. They must always, they decided, stand still while the airfoil was having the wind thrown at it, lest they budge the air in the room. And they must always stand still in the same spot.

They did not know, but their pulses did, their prophetic airborne souls, that a time would come when the watcher over the experiment could upset things merely by letting a human gaze fall upon the infinitesimal mote being tested. Peeking spoils the flow of electrons. In other words, we get purity only when we look away. What's seen gets slewed. Science becomes, if it can, the indefinably discreet swain of phenomena, surreptitiously confiscating the charm of the beloved object.

HELEN KELLER HOLDING
MARK TWAIN

Rough to my touch, he talks on like a little factory between my arms, almost as if telling the story in his sleep and letting me get it as best I can with my eyes closed like his perhaps. The two boys, I think, caught fish, they fished for fish, and Mr. Twain he smells of pepper and mothballs. Maybe he has been stored away and they fetched him out for me. Maybe they say fitched instead. All the breath behind his words has warmth in it, coming right up from his heart, his lungs. His breath, the warmed air that was within him, comes up to the top like the fish to the two boys, who also tell each other stories, for all I know about boys fishing. Mr. Twain, he leaves things out. Did they sleep first or swim? They swim to keep from feeling sleepy, and I feel his voice rumbling long before it arrives at my hands, like a train from afar, from a very distant frost-sharp Russia down in him deep, where the boys have to break the ice to go fishing. They will always want to fish together, I have discovered that much from his story. And swim. Then sleep. Swim and sleep all at once as you can do if you are me, a flummoxed lady, but the right age for him, he says, putting all his trust in my thumbs. Now the two boys are on their backs looking up at the stars, but neither they nor Mr. Twain tell me how many there are or how close together they can get. Surely what they call prose, although invisible, could help us guess at such things. The boys are on their backs on the ground not on their backs in the still, big river, and they hush, although Mr. Twain's chapped lips do nothing of the kind. Straw surrounds his mouth, smaller straw his eyes. I see it is possible to find other names for hair. I am holding his voice, I am inhaling his mind, and we chuckle together when the story pauses for the boys to kind of snigger, as boys do. Nothing new in that. What is new, to me, is how the story is full of air, not wrapped up tight with cord, but full of bedsheets not yet slept on. There are whole sections when it is not itself and you are free, if anyone is, to think about buckets full of that big, still river water, to set by your feet and dip into, and then I understand that these gaps mean that you are always having to wait for boys, who do not measure their lives by alarm clocks and might be content to float along on that river for all their days, so long as the days all came after one another and not all at once like the words of some. Mr. Twain made this up, older than I, sort of mumbling it to me as if he were afraid of something like a lot of honey spinning around after him in a blizzard rough as all the scrubbing brushes in the world. So long as he can tell me about the two boys, over and over, he thinks he will be spared, the river his talisman, but I doubt that kind of metaphor's effect on what's roughly ephemeral. If I could, I would save him from young women who do not know he is a boy still and wants to lie on the river with them in never-ending mighty good weather.

ENRIQUE GRANADOS

We never knew we were living in a *Goyesca,* one of those brutal tableaux supposed to teach you what life is like, but more truly the badge of a violent temper. Drowning, we knew we just could not be drowning. It felt so smooth; surely we had to be doing something else, such as loving or dreaming or hearing the piano tuned. When you drown, you do not hear the music you have written, even if everything else comes back like a vomit of cinders.

Goyescas did well in Manhattan, the town that terrified us, she and I hunched in our skyscraper like two resuscitated Aztecs, with the money-belts itching our waists. Only room service knew us. Banks never. We had to get the money home to Spain and then never go anywhere else again. Something kept happening to us, though, wherever we were. On *The Sussex,* too, as it went down with its torpedo and I saw her flailing in the sea I jumped into.

Something was always happening. We could never sit back and enjoy what never happened.

E. J. BELLOCQ

Dubbed "Papa," he spoke in a high-pitched voice, staccato, and when he got excited he sounded like an angry squirrel. He waddled, ducklike; was only five feet high; had an enormous head, narrow shoulders, a bulky rear end, and fair hair. Unsociable in the extreme, he could on occasion be tempted to discuss photography, but he was forever afraid of being teased about his build. He took no interest in sports, theaters, galleries, and restaurants, or even in women—except as company with whom to chat. "He always behaved nice," says Adele. "You know, polite." But she also points out that "he done a few months in the ice house, so you can't tell." What is clear is that he lived at an economic level rather higher than the half-a-nickel of red beans, half-a-nickel of rice, that Louis Armstrong recalls his mother making and which you could also get along with soup and a beer at the Olympic Saloon on the corner of Canal and Royal for five cents. He had a Bantam Special; he once tried repeatedly to photograph a streetcar painted red, white, and blue but never got it entire; and his biggest fun, we gather, was standing on Canal Street with his exposure meter taking readings. He retired in 1938 and spent his last years just walking round the block or lolling by the water cooler at the Eastman Kodak Company on Canal Street, his cap falling off when he dozed. He dropped dead on Common and Carondelet, and everyone seems to think he had the Bantam Special on him when he fell. As for the Storyville portraits, they might have been a commercial assignment but are almost certainly, as John Szarkowski suggests, "a personal adventure"— "They possess a sense of leisure in the making, and a variety of conception not typical of photographic jobs done at the customer's request." Clearly, he found the women of Storyville compelling, and they knew he was extolling them in a unique way.

All of the women are lovely, which is extraordinary; some are nude, which is not; and some are dressed up as if going to church, which is ordinary or extraordinary depending on your point of view. Number One is a thick-handed girl with a top parting and a severe hairdo who smiles with her eyes as well as her mouth; she is quite oblivious of her bare bosom. There follows a brilliant study (improved by a stain that creates phantom raincoats hanging on the door) of a bashful wench dressed all in white as if for a garden party standing between the door jamb and a bedstead on which another girl is sleeping. A jolly Norman milkmaid in fancy pantaloons grins edifyingly with a dog on her knee. Eyes downturned, a long-haired brunette adds swollen-looking roses to her overblown front. Prone on a shawl draped over an ironing board, another girl looks into a poodle's eyes while cocking up one leg. One in a tight necklace against a messed white backsheet clasps her hands in her lap above a fractionally visible inch of suspender belt. A nude follows, posed on a couch against a locked door, whereas next is a prim girl with roses and a watch locket, stationed in front of a high hedge, dressed like a village librarian. Another, before a screen, sits on a stool, regal and patient, lacking only a piano. Here is one in gold beads, an undervest and black knee-stockings; a calm-faced one stands on a figured carpet, buxom and bold. A sullen one pouts away sideways as if she's already seen her successor, a curly-haired beauty who relaxes nude on a white divan against an interior chiaroscuro of a hospital-looking bed.

Number Seventeen is all striped stockings, at her side a bottle of Raleigh Rye on a table whose lower shelf is crammed with miniature chairs. Next, on a basketwork divan, a girl who looks like an elongated apricot; one with dog and lace cap, seated upon a trunk shoved against a besmeared wall; a chunky nude leaning against a chest of drawers as if examining the sea from the rail of an ocean liner; a deeply pensive one in a feather boa who might just have finished reading all of Edith Wharton; a nude in shoes against unpainted clapboards, her face all casual amiability. Later, an abstracted-looking girl in a total body stocking—a gymnastics coach taking ten; a fat one aghast at her own face in the dressing table mirror, with

69

a pennant saying East something-or-other on her right; then a cordial creature in eye mask and knee stockings, her sharp-pointed forefinger aimed down at the divan; followed by the earthy diffidence of a nude who seems to be waiting for Godot with one knee frozen to a chair.

And a shock at the end: an extraordinary nude whose head has been obliterated, wearing a black G-string, a pacifier in her navel, her bosom scalded white and striated, her right shoulder cut up into chunks without falling apart, and—around her—squirts of lightning, which are score-marks on the plate. The room seems to disintegrate around her while she prods one hand into the air at waist height. It's like an auto-da-fé done by a misogynist with a stylus and some nitric acid.

BARON VON RICHTHOFEN

One day not long before his "gentlemen" observed
Him glide his triple-winger, dead, beyond the lines
The British held, baronial heart in body's cockpit
Seeping red the color of his Fokker 425,
His by-appointment jeweler ran out of silver
For making cups, and the baron ordered no more:
Sixty cups for sixty toppled sitting ducks,
Crammed on the shelves in his ascetic room,
Only made it glinting-bare;
Convexly met his silver sneer
Like urns
Paraded in thin air.

A manual of war he then sat down to write,
A promptbook for air circuses in wars to come,
His dreams like slowly foaming bombs, his face aflame,
His ribs in red-hot harness curling to release

Balloons of lungs that soared above his flying pyre
While Manfred melted, only the Von asbestos,
Hard-assed as a silver sporting cup and pliable
As crystal. His dog he called Moritz. His father
Didn't show emotion. Their familial cross
Was iron and their serfs were crass
Inferiors
In trench entrenched or *Schloss*.

Odd? Of course. Lieutenants in the Uhlan Lancers
Rode and hunted, stalked and shot wild pig or bison,
Foxes, elk, and birds. But a gentlemen who preys
On his own kind, being cruel to be kinder
Than mere faceless gunners on the ground, must have had
A setback early on. He did. An iron gong,
Third Class, for galloping, is not a First in Greats,
Nor transfer to the infantry (the Office of Supply)
An accolade. And so he wrote: "It's wrong
For me to be collecting cheese and eggs among
These Belgians. I'm a Von,
I ought to fly: I'm almost like a king."

That did it, although not in full. We must remember
How observers, then, were aristocrats, and pilots
Only sergeant-chauffeurs. He was back-to-front
Or, rather, second in the tandem in the tube

74

Called fuselage. And it wasn't even war at first,
Opposing airmen swapping friendly waves and hi's,
Then later taking pot-shots in a boyish way
With rifle or revolver in the upstairs wind.
One Russian with a ball and chain took shies
At enemy propellers. How unwise:
The chain rebounding
Nipped his throat; the ball beat out his eyes.

The pilots flew in parallel like friends, a code
Observed while observers shot themselves to bits
In paltry broadsides in midair. Both armies laughed
And Baron Von said, "*Ach,* the pilot cannot kill,
Observers cannot steer." And so to aeroschool
He went and terrorized the wild pigs while on foot.
His solo was a travesty: he crashed and failed,
And kept on failing, simply couldn't qualify,
So gave the local pigs more hell, yelled *Blut*
And *Feuer* and always ate his arrowroot.
One day he passed,
Disliking sky and planes but deadly keen to shoot.

His ship flew, he knew not why; his engine churned,
A mystery to him. He'd never probed the bowels
Of his horse: it ran, it leapt, and so should this.
Already, as observer, he had shot one Frenchman down

But had not been accredited; and now—his Albatross
Equipped with pilot's gun (pretentious and absurd,
All felt)—he downed his second, none believing
He could do this thing while piloting a plane.
Then Tony Fokker saved him with the gun that fired
Between propellers, missing blade by blade;
The baron met ace Boelcke on a train
In August of '16. The ace-to-be was made.

In late October Boelcke fell, colliding in midair,
So Manfred carried on the cause, his only
Handicap his dwindling span (he'd only twenty
Months to come). As killers go, he played for safety;
Three-quarters of his targets were reconnaissance
Two-seaters, blind as bats beneath the flimsy tail.
The sun, that killer's aide, he kept behind him,
Sent subordinates for trophies to the wrecks
And wouldn't grace his victims' funerals
Or meet the wounded in the hospital.
So private he became
The French declared him not an *homme* at all

But a heavy-leathered feminine, a joke he heard
But could not see. The maimed got boxes of cigars
To smoke themselves to death with, behind screens,
And said the Von was tops—unlike his brother Lothar

(Both a pilot and a lech)—who flew at Manfred's side
And angered him by being frivolous.
"I kill and I feel cool a quarter of an hour,"
Said senior to junior Von, "a peace most soldierly.
But you, you have no peace at all: you louse up
Life and death. Your shooting is promiscuous,
Your lust is trigger-happy.
But we're few, so even you're of use."

How right the baron was: the Boelcke squadron,
Twelve in all, were halved in six mere weeks;
A seventh lay abed with wounds, while eight and nine
Went off their heads with nerves. The baron rallied
What remained and led them with distinction,
Making three sorties per day until they fizzled out;
And one day he himself, force landing on the lines
Of his own countrymen, was met with gentle jeers
For coming down at all. Aloof, he opened up his coat,
Suppressed an antipatriotic thought
And put some hubris in his gaze:
For there it hung, Blue Max, *the* medal, at his throat,

And all sank to their knees to honor him. *Oberleutnant*
He was soon to be, and *Rittmeister* thereafter
At about a thousand bucks a year until he died,
Bequeathing four great rules to those he'd singled out

For glory with him: Know mount, know mount of foe,
Know wind and sun, and be belligerently shrewd.
Embarrassed by his fame (the bands at railroad terminals,
The girls in white who pelted him with petals),
He bowed and clicked, and massacred for running nude
Whole droves of forest pigs, with no thought of reward.
But on his birthday (twenty-five)
The kaiser called him up, invited him to feed.

On and on he flew, caught frostbite, cramped his knees,
Agreed to put on shows for generals-on-a-visit,
The killer-baron from Silesia enacting how
It's done, his only prop (beside what sucked him on)
A solitary Sopwith or an FE2,
For butterfly while he played wasp. A-zoom he went
In double scissors, Immelmann or solar plunge,
Red seed in those binoculars of Zeiss and lens.
A Jack-the-Bonestalk climbing up his plant,
He climbed to kill and not to stunt,
A trigger
Custom-fitted where the firing button went.

His girls? We do not know. Maybe one died of love,
Anonymous and pure in a Westphalian *Schloss;*
A nurse, they say, who'd stanched his bleeding brainpan,
Trepanned herself to death because his noble blood

Was antiseptic and he always wore black gloves
When touching women, silver, or the banisters at home.
He switched from camouflage to enemy-provoking red,
Permitting all his "gentlemen" this color-spree
As well, provided they commingled it with chrome
Or some subordinating shade. His only claim
Was to identity;
That scarlet triplane was his *Lebensraum*

In which his basic shyness could not show, or fear
Invade him at a gibe he couldn't parry.
Wounded, he was found and sent to Brest Litovsk
To witness peace talks with the Bolsheviks, whereas
One French ace, lost and never found, was reputed
To have flown away so far he breasted the horizon
Like a winner at the tape and streamered it behind.
Thus comets come and aces go; astrologers keep score.
All headaches and maturing pain, the baron
Now devised his circus, vaunted supersquadron
To annihilate the British,
Killing while he made them grin.

His pilots, in their teens, he told to look behind;
A bullet in the rear meant death, certainly dismissal.
And so, before returning to the drome, they landed
In the fields to patch up what the bullets had gone through

Like dandies mopping off a lipstick stain or extra-
Sweetening the breath. April 20 (still '18) he downed
Lieutenant Lewis, victim number eighty; waved
To him, as he flew by, in bland comradeliness,
And next day ended his career. The war was stunned:
Exactly who had triggered off the lead that canned
This eagle extraordinary
No one knew. Whoever had, had sinned.

After his death, in toast to "our most worthy enemy,"
Lieutenant-ace Rhys-David (twenty Huns) informed
His fellow pilots, "Anyone would have been proud
To have killed Richthofen in action, but" (be fair)
"Would also have been proud to shake his hand alive."
It wasn't tact or sham; it may have been adoring;
It's certainly exemplary to those who love their hate
And *ode* their *ammo,* who didn't know a gentlemanly
Bullet kills you less than vulgar firing
Squads or the 1918 Richthofen Wing
Commanded, as it came to be,
By all of Hermann Goering

Who went political at length and dressed in white,
His paunch a bunker, cloth-of-gold, bemedaled, firm.
But not Richtofen, though, whose major of a father
Rejoined the colors for the war, whose cousin Frieda

80

Left her professor for a priapist,
A David Herbert whose lifelong abhorrence
Was fancy-talking folk and fancy ways
Except for those with daisies in their private hair
And sallow urchins in the streets of Florence.
The baron lost his war through chance,
Might otherwise
Through chivalry have cooked the Belsen mince.

Postmortem by three doctors made it sure. They laid
Him out in state, then, in a suitable chateau
Where flying-men could come to pay their last respects
Before the funeral's military drum, six pilots
Carrying the coffin of "our brother, Manfred,"
As the British chaplain reckoned him, while officers
Lined up to give a last salute. The firing party
Fired and toasts were drunk that night, only Mannock,
Noted ace, refusing to join in novices'
Blithe games conducted in upholstered Messes.
War was war to him,
And not a grail for well-bred glosses.

But there was more to come, and better; the RAF,
At only three weeks old, flew over German lines
To drop a canister that held a photograph
Of Von's last resting place (Manfried, they wrote,

Misspelling as the military do when sad);
The flowers, black or white, could all be seen
Expressing no opinion on that narcissistic mound;
The firing party had returned their guns to slope;
The Allies nothing sordid or in any way unclean
Did on that military, decent scene;
The Germans later
Reinterred the baron in Berlin.

SIR EDWARD ELGAR, 1920

They do not believe it when they see it, having been admitted to peer at me: the derivative composer of works noble, dignified, and beautiful, reduced to crouching here at the billiard table over a microscope, as if the lens tube held the secret of her death. Somehow, to make death small, I magnify the tiny: a skewed logic, perhaps, but I was never one for logic.

Now I peer at dust, hair, a flake of dandruff, a touch of spit, and nothing seems melodious at all. No one calls me Edoo any more; I was Edward to the Edwardians, Edoo to her. All I hear now is the soft throb of an ocean liner's engines, but I am not at sea. Oh but I am. I once played her part of something new, and she approved, except of one passage, which made her tauten her lips and go rather grim. Next morning I found a little piece of paper pinned over the offending bars, on which she had written, "All of it is beautiful and just right, except this ending. Don't you think, dear Edward, that this end is just a little . . . ?" It is.

SIGMUND FREUD
AT SIXTY-SIX

When you want a wrong opinion, find a quack. When you cannot stand to know the truth, go to some gross inferior. This is called denial. Then let him carve away at your jaw and palate as if he were making a sandwich in some Viennese delicatessen.

There I was, bleeding to death on a soiled cot in a tiny room, while, stuck in the trench the quack had left in my mouth, a vague retarded dwarf fidgeted and whined. The grotesque bulb of his head wobbled about. And he shouted for a nurse because he was drowning in a tide of my freshly minted blood. Puss in Boots I called him.

After the nurse bustled me out of there, I had to think again, obliged to want an opinion that was right. Rhinologist number two said, "*Ach,* Herr Doktor Freud, one dies just as finally from unknown, or unadmitted, truths as from their opposite. Not to wish to die is merely to misinterpret a dream. The death wish is nothing but a state of mind. As for the cigar that graced your mouth, might it not have been safer in your other end, where, although the gasses are flammable, the wind flows outward only?'' When I need another opinion, I will ask for it with that very same below-stairs mouth. I will ask the dwarf.

FREDERICK DELIUS

It was I who taught the world how to dream another dream while already dreaming. Destined for the wool trade, I persuaded my father to set me up on an orange plantation in Florida. Already I was dreaming how my oranges would rot while I went out on alligator hunts and canoe trips, in the course of which I dreamed of singing in the choir of a synagogue and teaching music to decorous young ladies. At Grez, I converted aloofness into an art form, as one destined also to go blind will. When Jelka and I escaped to London, away from the German war, we had with us only one thing: a Gauguin, to look at which was like having the sun shine on my unseeing eyes later. I flailed my hands, I fidgeted like mad in my chair, I told Fenby my music. Called to England for a Delius festival, I gave them my mushroom-white face and my horn-rimmed glasses. Wadded in with cushions, I sat in my invalid chair and they carried me from the ship to the ambulance. A dreamer was coming home. During my music, I lay on a litter banked with flowers, just like a corpse, and during the concert they all watched me as if I were going to turn into a butterfly; but

I did not, I turned instead into a megaphone. I spoke my thanks. Had the king known how much morphine I was taking, would he have made me a Companion of Honour? Would Oxford have withheld its degree? I was sixty-seven, just like one of the ruins that Cromwell knocked about a bit. Whatever I was doing, and whatever they, in my deepest heart, where the oranges of syphilis grew and rotted, I was always being carried up the mountain in my bath chair so that the sun could blaze on my face like a disease. There is a rocking of small boats so loaded with flowers that they begin to fill with water and the topmost blooms float away, bonnets for sea snakes. My grave is lined with laurel leaves and lit with two hurricane lamps. I am buried in Limpsfield, near cuckoos and summer gardens. I was too limp, they said, some of them: too submissive, too slack, but they never understood. You do not need to be busy to fall to pieces, you need not be energetic in order to go to seed, to rot. I was always a white man in a community of the black. I was the chromatic addict of the trance, as Mrs. Belle McGhee Phifer saw. Only music and Florida are real. Come. Swoon with me as the flesh goes bad. We will wear petals where the scabs were and hold our lepers' hands up to the sun. The mass of life is a ritual quantity. Wolf it down. Be blighted with curds and whey.

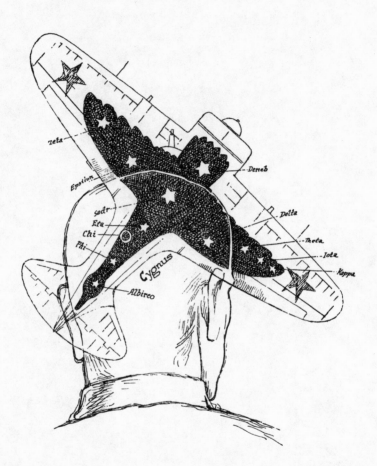

NIKOLAI POLIKARPOV

We showed them off first in the May Day fly-past over Moscow in 1935, loud and stocky, their bodies like tapered barrels. The Polikarpov I-16 was a reasonably fast and swift-climbing fighter, capable of 323 mph, and in the Spanish Civil War it often outmaneuvered the Messerschmidt Bf109Bs. *Ishak,* we named it: Little Donkey, its thick back strong for the rod. Twenty thousand little donkeys we had, all told, and I am proud (though not exactly gibbering with delight) to have designed it. Whenever I see the plan view of it, I see not an airplane but the constellation Cygnus, with the same stubby nose, straight leading edge to the wings, forward-curved trailing edge as if plucked voluptuously after it, except that the constellation has a longer, narrower fuselage, between Eta and Albireo anyway. Is Cygnus the plane of my dreams, not quite attained in my own design, but designable somewhere by someone? Am I thinking of the Thunderbolt or Spitfire, instead, whose trailing edges had that half-elliptical, rapturous curve? What I have forgotten is that there is no need, not even a reason, to draw Cygnus so beautifully; a crude simplistic cross would link up the stars. There is no swan up there, no little donkey down here. It is all in our minds where, when we fly, we are truly being flown.

EDITH SITWELL

Once upon a train her father lowered his copy of the *Times,* looked at her, shuddered, and shut her out again. As an adolescent she wore what she called her Bastille: one piece, both brace and corset, to remedy a curvature of the spine and weak ankles; the other a facial brace to straighten out her long tuber of a Plantagenet nose. Her specialist, a Mr. Stout, looked like a statuette made in margarine then frozen stiff. Perhaps she felt much the same when out walking in Eckington woods, made to wear a veil lest the locals see how like a leper she was. Truly hurt into poetry (and into witty sarcasm), she had pale gold hair that sometimes looked green and decided she must have been a changeling left behind by pranking fairies who took a human baby away with them. She was our first mutant muse. Those same locals she hid from in the woods decided she slept in a coffin and was really a vampire, flying with wings made from old umbrellas and the lost kites of little local boys. Her father wrote a famous history of the two-pronged fork but made a point of asking Sargent the painter to emphasize Edith's crooked nose when he painted her. Sargent straightened it instead and omitted her pet peacock, thus giving her the confidence later on, when pushed to go to local balls with her hair all frizzed and hauled down along and over her nose, to spurn the white tulle dress chosen by her mother and buy herself one of long black velvet. She was six feet tall. If you looked like a greyhound, she said, why try to look like a Pekingese?

At her most crocodilous, as she called it, she said of one poetaster critic that he examined the nature of groundsel and the sex life of the winkle and told someone else that she had just been defending him: "They said you weren't fit to live with pigs, but I said you were." Her histrionic acuity rarely faltered, perhaps because she warmed her head with a turban. Virginia Woolf said she looked like an ivory elephant. She, herself, after meeting Marilyn Monroe and Zsa-Zsa Gabor and the international stud Porfirio Rubirosa, said she felt she had been made for physical love but wept at never having known it. Her first love was an unresponsive Guards officer, her last the homosexual painter Pavel Tchelitchew; but her truest lover was the photographer Cecil Beaton, who made her lovely, finding her complexion fresh as that of an amaryllis, her eyebrows like tapering mouse tails, the noble forehead like tissue paper, her wrists like delicate stems, and her visage entire flooded with the mad moonstruck ethereality of a ghost.

SACHEVERELL SITWELL

If the Sitwells had not invented themselves, they would have been born in the usual way. Determined, as Sacheverell says, to "leave a mark," they did, Edith reciting "Façade" through a megaphone in 1923, Osbert debunking spiritualists, and Sacheverell—well, he was the quiet logistician, although he seems to have invented himself with an existentialist zeal beyond his sister and brother, like Kierkegaard "a Janus bifrons," laughing with one face, weeping with the other. In fact, not eccentric at all.

Their village, Eckington, was the one I was born in; theirs the shadow I grew up in, yet less a shadow than some albedo effect of reflected hypoliterary radiation, maybe a byproduct of Midlands smog. Impossible Plantagenet creatures of almost illicit leisure, they three haunted the edge of the village, occasionally passing among us yokels: Edith, the poet, opening a flower show like some stranded, hieratic cormorant; Osbert, like the military attaché to Lilliput, braying an august hallelujah as he strode. Stories abounded: epic, salacious, morbid, but Sacheverell (Sasha to us) showed up in few of them; something straight, subordinate, or unhistrionically pensive, exempted him. He had the best mind of the three. And the best-stocked.

For Want of the Golden City is a well of relaxed connoisseurship, an untidy but lavish mosaic, almost as if, after a lifetime's writing in the wake of older siblings, the author had decided to try on some such role as the Malraux of Renishaw, siting himself in the museum without walls that is the world of art, recapping indefatigable travels and listening (like the dog in the old HMV logo) for the Master's Voice, which never comes.

A grateful memoir, it's also an acid bath of hard-earned atheism. Time and again he says there is only this life, only man, only art, only evolution. "Much hardening of the sensibilities," he writes, "is needed before one can face the truth which is that there is nothing there." Face it he does (and in prose rarely as clumsy as that bit is), reviewing his lifetime's purposes all the more candidly for his not knowing those of the universe (if any) and facing himself for what he is: a patrician Brahmin who regrets writing too many books, but not his cosmopolitanism, his receptivity, or his *Angst*. The book begins with a sustained, creative account of a dying fly and, much farther on, sketches the last days of Arthur Waley, the translator of Chinese poetry, who refused painkillers to listen through his agony to Haydn string quartets.

This existential leitmotif, grounded in Sitwell's notion of *pourriture noble* ("noble rot" as distinct from athlete's or ple-

104

beian's foot), in part redeems even his snobbish disdain for longhairs and TV and the puzzled narrowness of his taste in music (no mention of Ives, Schönberg, Shostakovich, etc.). He goes down with all cannons blazing, sometimes exploding in his face, as when he laments the recognition of upstarts Pound and Eliot. The reverse face of his bigotry is his anger that a Van Gogh can't sell a painting in his own lifetime, that the BBC erases recordings of Yeats reading his poems while it promotes "the sales of disc-jockeys." To the absurdity Camus spoke of, he opposes a teleology of taste such as no man possesses in total but of which this Sitwell has more than his share. Against the rock-Huns with microphones, a Herrick devotee who dislikes Eliot is on the same side as the Eliotist, nonetheless.

But it's not only a heroic fastidiousness that occupies and ennobles his mind; he goes repeatedly, in both art and everyday, to emblems or epitomes of the absurdity that sends him to art—as if he has always to renew acquaintance with the original provocation. There is a superb chapter on gargoyles. Rembrandt's *Rat-Killer,* with his shelf of dead rats round his neck and his "quisling" rat attendant, exercises him deeply, as do Brueghel, Bosch, El Greco, and Avercamp, the deaf-mute painter whose figures turn their backs to us. Despite all man's accumulated finesse and amenity, the ultimate grotesqueness of his condition abides. The "For Want" of the title means you too.

One might have expected Sitwell therefore to turn to Magritte, Munch, or Schiele, say; but he doesn't, instead amassing first-hand evidences—portrait presences—of his own that surpass even those of art. Thus we get the microcephaloid of Dakar, with spiderbitten bags beneath his eyes; a row of pigs' heads in a butcher's window, one labeled "Dying to Meat You"; Matterig, the 1859 suicide who chopped off his hand before committing approximate hara-kiri; the Aztec ritual of the "Flayed One," in which the priests danced in the skins of freshly flayed captives; Carthaginians crucifying a lion; Baudelaire, doomed by syphilis, with his head shaven and shirtneck open, as if awaiting the guillotine; a notorious highwayman transported from the belly of a horse; a tramp in lady's lacesided boots, off which he'd cut the toes; the Jew found in an underground burial chamber in Jerusalem, crucified in the crouching position.

There are overlaps as well: Grock the clown is as frightening as any portrait of the demiurge; the "small, moronic head" of an elongated Christ by El Greco evokes that of a "mad beggar" repeatedly seen in Toledo. The gargoyles breathe; *Homo sapiens* is a gargling spout. In seeking to exorcize horror, or command it, Sitwell only implants it deeper within himself; and none of his articulately celebrated incidentals—blue bee-eaters on telegraph wires, Japanese whores with rolled-up mattresses, car lights at night like "astral stalking-horses," white truffles unearthed by "dogs with the diploma ECTR (School of Truffle Hounds at Roddi)"—distract him for long. Not even what he calls "therapeutic architecture." Not even all of Trollope. There is no "golden city," only wherever, under sentence of death, "one has been happy." What he calls this "*grande machine* of a book" entombs an exhilarated anxiousness which, as he brings out in the chapter called "VIP Lounge," may be all life is for. The last analysis is always incomplete.

AMY JOHNSON:
5 JANUARY 1941

Anyone who is a pilot is never only a pilot, but navigator, geographer, engineer, hermit, mystic, beloved explorer of God.

For once I didn't get it right. I opened the bag of the winds, and the winds knew me. Above fog without a radio, fuel gone, and nothing in sight, I am the true Pandora. I have to bail out like some inebriated mermaid. How quiet the down-swooning seems, almost as if nothing were wrong, like a wait in a solicitor's office. Only Amy would have risked it, they will say. I'll *smell* my way home, I said; I am ferrying a twin-engined *Oxford* back to Oxfordshire. What's more natural than that?

I was always a bit hamfisted when landing.

Take the night train, Amy. What? And sit all night on my parachute in an unheated corridor? Give me two Cheetahs any day, most of all when they add up to 740 horses. I love horses. Goodbye, *Jason, Jason II, Desert Cloud, Seafarer, Black Magic,* my only true beaux. I have only 2,550 hours or so, rather more than a hundred days. I am less than a third of one year old, then. This is the estuary of life. Let it be known that the groping hand that lifted aloft at the last was waving.

Amy means *friend* or *love*.

AMY BEACH

Another Amy, this, but also Marcy and, by maiden name, a Cheney too. She writes a *Mass,* an *Invocation,* and *Variations on Balkan Themes;* she composes all through the quarter-century of her marriage to H.H.A. Beach, a Harvard surgeon, hardly ever performing; and then, as if death has sprung a trap, she goes off to Europe to rest, but it is her own discreet way of gathering her forces up. She begins to pour into the public ear, does much of her composing at the MacDowell Colony, the Peterborough linnet. Among all her songs, *Ecstasy* does so well that she buys a summer home on Cape Cod with the proceeds, and it is this structure, seen in her mind's eye as a mosaic, meaning a work of the muses, put together not from bits of wood but squares of ecstasy: the ample gray slate roof, the pale purple-tinged blue of the clapboard walls, the white shutters to her celibate eye like millinery, the chocolate-brown outhouse with its high window as if double-floored, the pale olive of the garden as full of rhododendrons as a stave of notes. She is the first American woman to write a symphony and, for all her being one of the so-called Boston Classicists, she sometimes feels as if she is the only composing woman, the only muse of ecstasy, whose lineaments in daily life and the abstract mind she links to the flesh of which the heart is made. The heart too is a mosaic, whose tiny pieces all want to beat, in unison or not. Ecstasy unites her with everything: the lost, the won. She adores each and every snowflake in the snow. She is melody's aunt.

FRANK BRIDGE

Bluff and rather beefy, he had a mother-of-pearl soul. If ever there was a male muse of the country house whose empty terraces are thick with nostalgia, whose rooms echo with vows and protestations, whose wallpaper does not scoff at such words as *swain* and *tryst,* he was it, his hair tousled upward into a near-pompadour, his brown eyes aloofly evaluative behind pince-nez, his mouth almost hidden behind a downswept mustache of the kind Walter Pater pressed on cats like a wet brush when he kissed them on the mouth. Bridge looked prim, a Blimp in concert togs. That is the Bridge of the *Piano Quintet* and the Thomas à Kempis *Prayer.*

Yet the same man wrote *The Sea* without being in the least impressionistic or Debussy-like. He dealt in structures, not in atmospheres. Stealing from Richard Jefferies, he prefaced his *Two Poems* with a surprising remark: "Those thoughts and feelings which are not sharply defined, but have a haze of distance and beauty about them, are always the dearest." Not in Bridge, who abhors haze. His dead have exact faces. His nostalgic continuum gave way to something spiky without being acerbic, even while he steered away, as he always had, from the twin gods of British music: folk song and chorus. It was *The Sea,* conducted by the composer, that bowled over the eleven-year-old Benjamin Britten in 1924, yet Bridge came to despise the work, even the "Moonlight" section that had especially drawn Britten and about which Bridge had written a program note saying, "a calm sea at night. The first moonbeams are struggling to pierce through dark clouds, which eventually pass over, leaving the sea shimmering in full moonlight." One sees why he shrank from the verbal version, but not why he turned his back, or a cold shoulder at least, on the opulent poignancy of his early years. "Fancy," he used to joke, "a cellist always playing in tune," as the young cellist Florence Hooton did in his *Oration.* When Bridge writes for cello, the gods have a lump in their throats and things atonal are the barbed wire of a war that has not even begun. When it comes, this Fauré of the Suffolk Downs will volunteer.

VIRGINIA WOOLF
BY THE RIVER OUSE

I am going to flush myself away, an Ophelia of the middle class. Suttee voce. Odd how the mind never deserts you, even at the very last, when it is the thing that has condemned itself to go.

No more picnics, no more sun-mulled shrimp or heavy sherry trifle. No more peeking into the windows of London, when the saffron lamplight beckons and we stand on tiptoe, ogling the linoleum and the big pot rabbits full of fairground feathers. They eat with their sleeves rolled up, their elbows in the fingerbowls. They pick their noses while buttering their bread. They masticate from side to side, sliding the wodge of food across.

Well, here lies one whose books were writ in water. How may a flow appraise a flow? I would have been better off at the bottom of the Arno or shipwrecked with Shelley off Spezia. The mind is a surf, ladies. All else is a railway compartment full of Arnold Bennett. That is what has done me down, done me in: too many Brussels sprouts, too few visionary flight lieutenants.

I wanted a wedding cake made of snow, ice cream made from yaks' milk and pink. I wanted the bright beautiful refulgent day, not the sullen undertow that told me only: You are a woman and you will have to die. I do not thus like the initiative twisted from my hand. I go down the field with today's *Times* in my hand, to do something rich and strange to myself, and back I come, burbling for tea and scones, a yak, a crested warbler, a Beethoven with breasts, a Debussy with a womb, a Rodin with his period thick and musky on him, a Wagner in full flying menopause.

RICHARD HILLARY

Stuck in its groove, the new cockpit hood of Flying Officer Hillary's Spitfire will not budge. He and a ground crew work away with files and oil, but the hood slides only halfway when the order comes for Squadron 603 to scramble. A corporal crosses his fingers as Hillary taxis off.

Half an hour later the cockpit is aflame. The hood jams. Hillary tears off his straps, frees the hood, passes out, and comes to at 10,000 feet after falling out. He tugs the rip cord and parachutes toward the sea, where, afloat in his life jacket, he notices dead white skin coming off his hand. His lips bulge like tires, but soon he cannot see them at all, having gone blind. He loosens the valve of his Mae West so as to drown, but the chute buoys him up, and he starts to laugh, hallucinate, and dream. Hours later, the Margate lifeboat finds him, and as he thaws he begins to feel all of the pain of his burns. His agony, not that he calls it that, has only just begun.

All this happens in the six-page "Proem" or preface to *The Last Enemy,* first published in 1942 (in the United States as *Falling Through Space*) and now revived, as a classic of air warfare deserves to be. But the book is more than that, revealing how a smug and supercilious Oxford dilettante became a connoisseur of mortality, an authority on the softness of human meat in a world where the forces of "anti-life," as he called it, outdo those of good. He comes through as an absurdist of the dogfight, a silver-spooned baron of battle reduced by pain and rage and grief to the random guesswork of a pagan child. He yearns to get back into the air and shoot down more Huns, and he wants to write about not quite knowing what else to believe in; but he is dead at 23, himself shot down with his problem unsolved.

This is less a book based on tranquil recollection than it is a severe conspectus assembled during convalescence from heroic bouts of plastic surgery. Indeed, his convalescence ended only with his death in 1943. There was so little time. *The Last Enemy* quivers with fateful twists. On the last page he decides to be a writer, but he has already finished his only book. The proem, coming first, feels written last, then put up front as the stark premise to a flashback reconnaissance that catches up with itself at chapter six; you have to wait a hundred pages to see what happens after they get him to hospital and administer painkiller. In the proem he harks back to one of his early short stories in which the hero, having fallen from an ocean liner, calls for help (like Hillary in the North Sea) with a lone seagull for company.

So *The Last Enemy,* drafted as preliminary to a book that would really count ("I would write of these men") ends up as The Last Book, an unintended terminus, and Hillary's *beau geste* of flying against the Luftwaffe again, with ruined face, becomes a nonverbal epilogue. Nowhere in the book does he mention its actual writing under what must have been terrible circumstances, just as he never reveals what subject he had been studying at Oxford.

Here is another of those documents from within the inferno that bring into our ken almost unthinkable dimensions of reverse response: beyond hatred of suffering to hatred of sufferers, beyond hatred of evil to hatred of humanity itself, and beyond hatred to ecstatic paralysis. No wonder that Ernest Gann in his foreword to the St. Martin's edition, aghast at what Hillary endured as his face and hands were put together again (more or less), coins the phrase "the absolute rectum of despair."

Once read about, the eyes caked with gentian violet do not go away. Or the nurses who faint while changing his dressings. Or the beetles that seem to run down his face. Or the bloated prosthetic lips. Or the complex deliriums in which bacon, streptococci, Mercurochrome, eau de cologne, and exposed bone provide a context for the howls of a young girl. He dare not blow his nose lest he puff his grafted lip away. His arm, where the new lip came from, splits open like a fan, "exposing a raw surface the size of a half orange." A thin steel probe clears the hole behind his ear for drainage. The rest is septicemia, suppuration, Protonsil, and cold brown tea. His skin green-blue, Hillary ponders Charles II's apology for being such an unconscionable time dying.

Then, suddenly, he is out and about in his beloved London among crocuses, thinking up a play to be called *Dispersal Point*. A bomb falls. He helps to pull a dead child from the rubble. "I see they got you too," the mother says, then dies. "I wanted to seize a gun and fire it, hit somebody, break a window, anything. I saw the months ahead of me, hospital, hospital, operation after operation, and I was in despair." The reprieve of spring is over.

Vivid flying scenes counterpoint this calvary. The engine quits on his first solo cross-country, and again on his second. He learns that most Messerschmitt 109s execute a half roll and a dive, when attacked from behind; that a Spitfire's propeller is long and must be kept clear of the ground on takeoff; that the recoil of eight machine guns cuts his speed by forty miles an hour. And above all he learns "the uselessness of all aerobatics in actual combat." By choice, with known consequences, when he flies he wears his goggles up. His plane he calls *Sredni Vashtar*, after Saki's ferret: "His enemies called for peace, but he brought them death." He shouts German invective over his radio at German pilots, one of whom answers. At night he switches off his mind "like an electric light," but never in this mesmeric, death-laden, self-censuring book, in which, as an Oxford hearty, he rows in Germany against Hermann Goering's prize crews, and, only a year later, flies against their aerial counterparts at 30,000 feet. The prose often makes one pause while the gathering small sum of Hillary's days, 365 times twenty-three, streaks through it in headlong, honorable charge.

Rereading him recalls for me the time when, as a green young flying officer, not long down from the same university, I presented myself to the adjutant at the RAF base I had been posted to. He showed me one of those yard-wide group photographs, this one of buoyant young pilots all wearing their new wings. As far as he knew, he said, he was the only one of them still alive. I mentioned Hillary's book, and he said he knew it well. Yet, oddly enough, in the ensuing years, in all my conversations with scores of Battle of Britain and Bomber Command aces and heroes, I never heard Hillary's name again. They were more at ease talking about Johnnie Johnson and Douglas Bader, perhaps because Hillary comes too near the bone, goes beyond aerial exploits toward an unknown region of Being and Nothingness in which all humans sooner or later earn a battle ribbon. Hillary, the premature complete existentialist, versed in French and German traditions, and spouting Donne, Verlaine, Goethe, Newton, Leonardo, Auden and Isherwood, Pound and Eliot, was too much of an intellectual without ever being in any sense academic.

As J. B. Priestley pointed out in a review of *The Last Enemy,* that appeared promptly enough for Hillary to see it, the RAF prefers its heroes inarticulate, almost as if taking a hint from Erasmus ("of those that are slain, not a word of them"). Unable to countenance Hillary the idea man, his contemporaries and successors also missed the spectacle of the man of ideas ultimately not knowing what to think. For Hillary the mind was no better a problem solver than the Spitfire was a night fighter—"the flames from its own exhaust make the pilot's visibility uncomfortably small." To read Hillary now is akin to reading Gide or Camus. How un-English he became before his flame went out. He belongs to literature and not to any flag. The last word in the book is "civilization," and Hillary knew that it did not mean a feeding frenzy, although it often looked that way. Death, as his epigraph from Corinthians 15:26 asserts, is the "last enemy," but, as his book reveals, there are so many other enemies distracting us from it. That is why they exist. Aching to kill death itself, he died to kill its ghouls.

SOPHIE SCHOLL,
22 FEBRUARY 1943

One last cigarette, my Lord, as if tobacco were *your* sacrament, and they will manacle my hands behind me and lead me up a few stairs to the big locked door with the bulbous brass handle. As if I were being taken to the headmaster for a dressing-down. For chatter, or cheating in the Latin test. It will not be long now. All I hear is a rattle of keys. The tall narrow door opens inward, pulled, and two men with faces impersonal as raffia tug me toward them as if they have been waiting for me all their lives. Seven seconds is all it takes from the door's opening to the end. Now, lifted aloft, I fly like Saint Joseph, a thought-out sentence per second. Two. I am laid face down on the rack. Three. A small bridge of wood comes down over my neck. Four. What have I done? Five. I insulted the Führer. Six. Who was *he*? Seven. I have been misinformed. Eight. I feel quite well, waiting. Nine. It will be more than twelve. Ten. I saw the hose, the lidded basket. Eleven. I have been misinformed. Twelve. Thank God it never happened. I am aboard the train from Ülm, a daisy in my hair and carrying a wicker basket that holds a spice cake and one bottle of Mosel wine. I draw the blackout curtains and see a jar of marmalade, 250 grams of butter, some strudel. I am still in my student skirt and blouse.

SIMONE WEIL

Dogs bark at cripples and ghosts and in some ways Simone Weil was both. Not content with the pain she had from recurrent migraines, she sought out for herself starvation and heavy manual labor (both industrial and agricultural); she prayed for extra pain and even to become a total paralytic. One of the least earthly of women, she increasingly fixed her attention—that sapping, inductive, inventive field of force—on God and death, managing to experience epiphanies ("Christ came down, and He took me") and even to make death do her bidding in the Ashford Sanatorium in Kent in 1944.

Such an odd combination of masochism and *affabulation* (fantasticating a mystical experience) is bound to provoke even in the most open minded a few harsh misgivings about frustrated spinsters, algolagnia, and hatred of the flesh. And it is possible to read Simone Weil's account of Christ in person ("Sometimes we stretched out on the floor of the *mansarde* and the softness of the sun came down upon me") in almost the same way as we would one of Moravia's studies in adolescent eroticism. Irreverent as it may be to say it, she had a crush on Jesus.

Yet, of course, as Gustave Thibon and others noted, she winced away from physical embrace—at least until the day she forced herself to declare, with rather dotty braggadocio, "I like being kissed by men with moustaches. It stings!" Remove the sting and the kiss is nothing for Simone Weil. After she had told friends about actually being kissed by a coal trimmer in Barcelona, she burst into tears when one of them asked if the man was drunk. This tireless intelligence, who beat Simone de Beauvoir into second place in the Ecole Normale entrance examination, belonged to her own version of the human condition. Frustrated, ill at ease as a woman and disconsolate at being human, she was reassured only by extra suffering and convinced only by what she thought God had told her. It is no wonder she became a kind of amateur saint and a successful suicide.

The photographs mutely record the decline from her second year, when she was chubby-cheeked, with curly black hair the color of her almond-shaped eyes—a pensive, cute doll—to thirty-four, when she starved herself to death in order to share the sufferings of the French. Her face in 1936 (at twenty-seven) is handsome, firm, full-mouthed and rather appealing; and in the uniform of Confederación Nacional del Trabajo she looks like an Arab youth dressed up for a baggy-trousered prank. But five years later she has an expression of intent vacuity. She has become the headmistress type, owl-eyed through excessive perusal, her expression an odd blend of hennish timidity and impatient pity. And there is a general look of—well, dryness. A sad little gallery of pictures indeed.

Astute and tomboyish, she chain-smoked and even rolled her own cigarettes. Because she did this carelessly she often had shreds of tobacco in her mouth. She wore large horn-rimmed spectacles for myopia, walked awkwardly in a forward lean, preferred clothes of masculine cut and low-heeled shoes. She "had a sharp, restless glance" and spoke in a staccato monotone, aspirating almost all her h's. She played women's rugby and would return from the fray covered with mud and bruises; and it was on her return from a game in 1930 that she had by far the worst attack, up to then, of her migraines (later attributed to sinusitis).

Among action shots these are the best: Simone Weil picking plums in the country and getting stranded on a high wall; hiding herself and her cigarette behind a Russian newspaper at staff meetings in school; on paydays at the Renault works treating herself to a package of cigarettes and some stewed fruit; digging potatoes for ten hours a day; insisting on carrying bundles of thistles in the wheat fields; helping (?) Marcel Lecarpentier on his thirty-foot, eight-ton fishing boat; exclaiming over the photo of some brawny tough, "That's my kind of man!"; giving away so much of her schoolteacher's salary that she went a whole winter without heat; burning herself while welding; asking a peasant if she might drive his plough and at once overturning it; scalding herself with oil while cooking for the CNT in Spain; aiming her rifle at an airplane that dropped a small bomb; neglecting to wash hands before milking cows; refusing a cream cheese because Indochinese children were starving; actually becoming a member of a *résistance* group that was a German trap; and, later, on her way to New York by way of Morocco, handing Gustave Thibon her notebooks on the station platform in Marseilles with a kind of absent-minded abruptness; thanking Father Perrin, her spiritual mentor, for never humiliating her; wandering in Harlem and attending a Baptist church there every Sunday ("I'm the only white person in the church"); studying folklore and quantum theory at the New York Public Library; asking Simone Deitz, who acceded, "Would you like to be my friend?"

She returns to Europe, playing volleyball on the way over and even dressing up on one occasion as a ghost. Finally she discovers a haven, during the thick of the air raids, at 31 Portland Road, London, and lives on black coffee; coughs all the time; refuses to look after herself or be looked after; strews papers all over her room; commends the good humor of the British, the pubs, the police system; wanders regularly into Hyde Park; and even elects to sleep out in the rain on the grounds of a convent. She tries to learn to drive; she deliberately upsets herself and Simone Deitz from their boat into the Serpentine. She sets herself a Benjamin Franklin-Jay Gatsby type of regimen: "avoid all loss of time . . . sleep on the floor or on a table in order to limit the hours of sleep to four

140

or five. . . ." Desperately eager to be parachuted into France, she occupies herself with the English metaphysical poets, her work for the Free French Ministry of the Interior, and the composition of *The Need for Roots*. At last, too weak to lift a fork, and refusing a pneumothorax as well as deciding against baptism, she is moved from the Middlesex Hospital to Ashford. The death certificate said, "Cardiac failure due to myocardial degeneration of the heart muscles due to starvation and pulmonary tuberculosis. The deceased did kill and slay herself by refusing to eat whilst the balance of her mind was disturbed." Perhaps, though, her mind's disturbance balanced for the first time. The certificate of burial reads, "Conducted own service—Catholic—French Refugee—Depth: 6 feet."

What else can we do, however uneasy or inferior we feel, but admire her passionate, sometimes maladroit devotion to the working class, her intense and unsectarian religious zeal, her capacity for self-denial, her attempt to convert pain into something wholly fruitful, her brilliant disruptive mind and painstakingly trenchant prose, her audacity in teaching the young, her almost peasant simplicity in aphorism, her refusal to defer to evil wherever she found it, her will, her guts, her crabbed truthfulness? We admire, but with a hunch that much of it amounts to a frenetic displacement of womanhood. Something crackpot emerges alongside what is her evident genius and her almost pernicious goodness.

Not that we don't respect the person—whether writer, say, or doctor—who uses the self as raw material. But Simone Weil, ostensibly on the side of life to the extent of justifying all of it, was really on the side of death; and her achievement, such as it is, implies the abandonment of the last, inalienable human privilege: the privilege of saying, "I loathe such and such a part of being human—say the small child with cancer of the clitoris, the child born deformed, the ugly and hardly quellable agony in which many people die, the obvious lack of divine justice—and I will not, much as it might be comfortable to be able to do it, involve myself in schoolmen's casuistries just to praise a pattern I did not invent."

What we make of her—this Jew, born a stoic and raised an agnostic, who gravitated to the godhead by using her magnificent brain to construct what George Herbert in her favorite stanza calls "a full consent"—depends on how far skepticism erodes our tolerance of experiences so private they cannot be appraised at all. Whereas the "system" of Teilhard de Chardin seems an inane wish fulfillment garbed as optimism, Simone Weil's embraces the whole pain of being—not just of bureaucracy (it "*always* betrays"), of war (never a means of liberation), humiliation (the worker enslaved to a mass-producing machine), and force ("It makes a man a thing"), but of man's total biological, chemical, and metaphysical state. She seems a Cleopatra, hugging the asp. Her best books (*Gravity and Grace, Waiting for God, The Need for Roots*) constantly shock us with their sustained, oblique obviousness.

She could not always be reached. She was too busy reconciling poles expressed in these two statements:

> We wish to uphold not the collectivity but the individual as the supreme value.
>
> [We] owe our respect to a collectivity, of whatever kind—country, family or any other—not for itself, but because it is food for a certain number of human souls.

And when she was not doing that she was pursuing her own *ascêsis,* asking to become as defective "as an old man in his dotage" and, like Samuel Beckett, linking up with "the poor, and the maimed, and the halt, and the blind." When she died, "Alain" would not believe it. "It's not true," he said, "surely she will come back!" Simone Weil herself said: "If there is something in afterlife, I shall come back. If I don't come back, it will mean that there is nothing." Which, really, is the endgame to beat all.

COUNT CIANO, 11 JANUARY 1944

Waiting here to be tried in order to be shot, I am a true gentleman of Verona. I, as distinct from my sedulously kept diaries, am of no worth, not even as a sample of *homo decadens*. Just a jumped-up playboy, I, married to Mussolini's daughter, my beloved Edda, who slaves night and day to keep her ponderous papa from having me tied to a chair and shot between the shoulder blades, befitting a traitor. I have been suave, sly, amorous; a man who refined gesture to the point of articulate language, as if fine-tuning a whole epoch for the deaf.

Well, Edda, Papa does not relent. I have no pride, no core, bedding down even in jail with my lady interrogator from the SS. We dance and smirk. Uttering for the last time the dearest four names in my life, I drink the vial of cyanide, but my SS lady, who loves me, has filled it with water, and all I do is choke. He must die four times, Hitler said, and I am doing it. I got to the top of the world so fast. Life was a tour of mellow brothels. Thank God I wrote it down, how the butchers arranged to carve up Europe like a haunch of sugar-dusted wedding cake while Ciano, that mouse of the indelible, hovered for crumbs. All I will ever be is those neatly dotted i's.

A priest leans over my shoulder, telling me that God wants me to forgive *Il Duce,* whom I curse and then forgive in the same breath. Behind my back, as ever, the innocent take aim and hold *their* breath. I am shaking the chair over. They steady it. This was not such a bad old world to wait for death in, Edda. They are giving us time to pray. No blindfold, no. What are they thinking of? Need the back of the head sham blind at the end? Or sight? Sham anything? This is the final entry, unwritten: Pen nibs stab my shoulder blades. Flash of daylight still. *Coup de grâce?* The world has not ended yet. But my charm is dead. Never mind what I used to say. Victory finds a hundred orphans, but defeat is a father.

ANTOINE DE SAINT-EXUPÉRY

Only a few feet above the runway, he sees the ground lights vanish and knows there is something big right in front of him. Captain Saint-Exupéry pushes forward on the stick. The plane nosedives, its wheels hitting hard, then rebounds back into the air over a truck that is carrying, of all things, a spare floodlight. Tonight, though, the floods are out while the pilots of Group 2/33 practice night landings. The only lights are faint, there to reveal the landing axis. Saint-Exupéry has saved his life (his copilot's and the truckdriver's) by doing something he learned when flying airmail before the war. It is January 12, 1940. There are no stars.

He hates the twentieth century, not so much for its ingenuities as for its materialism, its conveyor belts, its lack of pride in its agrarian, pastoral heritage. In fact he is something of a Luddite, this would-be combatant who complains that his fellow fliers mollycoddle him because they think his white beard will get tangled among the controls of his Lockheed Lightning photo-reconnaissance ship. He is, all through his letters, touchy, acerbic, lyrical, lonely, a poet of the stratosphere who, long before the notion becomes fashionable, realizes that we all live on the same small planet with nowhere else to go.

Here he is, looking back on a prewar crash landing in Libya; refusing to fly bombers; forgetting to switch on his electrically heated flying boots at 35,000 feet; noting that, where you breathe ice, breath turns into thin needles inside the oxygen mask; inventing and patenting an altimeter device; stealing a four-engine Farman at Bordeaux and flying forty young pilots to continue the war in North Africa. Illness dogs him. An old injury to a bone near the optical nerve makes his eye flare up. Wood splinters from a 1923 crash have given him septicemia. Inexplicable fevers beset him. He goes off to America, where he fumes, and then he returns to Europe aboard a troopship, talking incessantly to a Jungian psychiatrist. He takes a drink with a couple of bargemen. He eats fried fish and creamed chicken. Within the space of one year, he changes base twelve times (Morocco, Tunis, Algiers, Casablanca, Naples, Alghero, and so on). On August 1, 1943 he has engine trouble, overshoots the field, and slightly scrapes a wing. He slips on some stairs and breaks his back. Recovered, and flying over Annecy, he has mechanical trouble at the precise moment he turns forty-four, pursued by German fighters. Only the day after telling this to a friend in a letter, he goes up again, for mapping east of Lyon, and does not come back.

He notes the pathetic nature of the plane, how vulnerable it is: something between contraption and greyhound. A man can explode at 35,000 feet but never enter into another person. He loves wood fires and icy beds. Disliking too many creature comforts, he prefers his lodgings to evoke that atmosphere of the bear hunt. In his frequent vein of manual voluptuousness, he insists that the carpenter should plane his board as if it were essential to the earth's rotation. He dreams of money bankable only on Sirius and of one soft wave at Estoril, rolling into the bay like a ball dress out of season. He envisions the universe showing its goodwill through us. The condensation of the nebulae, the hardening of the planets, the formation of the first amoeba, and the colossal task of nature from the emergence of the amoeba to man. He deplores a generation with no spiritual values beyond the bistro, mathematics, and the Bugatti and yearns for the monastery of Solesmes. He considers weeping against a tree and writes in a petulant rage.

He seems almost to be cracking up in at least a tenth of his letters, but he always bucks up again, assigning himself a complex puzzle in math or changing his mind about high altitude—he likes it because it's uncluttered; he dislikes it because it's empty. Thinking of Vichy France, he decides that an organism creates its own anal passage. A sweetheart seen through a microscope "is merely an expanse of gritty surface," but soon after, in an X-ray of his spine, he can see the morning mists of a Japanese landscape. Rather stoically for a man who gets constant bad medical attention, he writes, "There is a friendly element in pain." He thinks of Sirius yet again (one's "inner climate" as seen from the star). Individuals bore him. What he longs for comes in flashes only, and one of these is double, of reconnaissance flight, seen first as a prowl for a virus on the body of France, then as a separation from all reasons for living—"illuminated by sunlight, and nevertheless more inaccessible than any Egyptian treasures locked away in the glass cases of a museum." He must once, he thinks, have been a Merovingian king. In Paraguay, the rain forest is always putting up a blade of grass between the paving stones of the capital city. His mind drifts.

Even as he scribbles things down, his image of the super-cockpit becomes a tent or a whitewashed room he calls a dovecote, in which he pulls throttles, far above the planet of the telephone, thus evading the anthill of the future. "I prefer," he says, "to be a gardener," but it is as the oldest fighter pilot in the world that he disappears in 1944.

CLAUS VON STAUFFENBERG

Here is a Hitler-head, the whole face a pinkish box, the dank hair combed through to either side with the white scalp showing (a barbed-wire pocket comb has passed through here). The mustache is a black kempt hedge beneath which gapes the spellbinding purple mouth, toward which—and this is what staggers me—Stauffenberg marches maimed, in his one good hand a briefcase bomb with a big honest clock on the outside.

He is going to plant the bomb in Hitler's mouth, not under the map table, like some old barrel organ exploding. There is going to be deluge of monkey fat interspersed with bits of noble Von, almost like those old rituals of the bloodthirsty ancient Greeks.

This time, Stauffenberg will have gone up with his own balloon. It was the only way ever to do it. Somebody has been paid to read my novel and illustrate my mind, and I am willing to believe anything when I see that bruised and livid sky behind the bunker, stretched out like a membrane unwrapping hell.

But the dapper, mutilated colonel remains as frozen, in his brave repeat, as the lovers on Keats's Grecian urn. He keeps his back to us, on this novel's jacket, until the smack of doom.

WILHELM CANARIS

Like Hitler, he had little private life, although married with two daughters. Hitler and he respected the domestic aridity they felt in each other. They both kept on the move, if only to flee the paperwork they abhorred, and their women. They doted on dogs. And when they were closeted together they overlapped so much that they never saw each other plain; when they finally did, Canaris saw the lethal cynic Hitler really was, and Hitler the dissembling plotter Canaris had become. On April 5, 1945, Hitler was shown Canaris's private diaries and had him hanged on the ninth, only three weeks before he shot himself. Weirdly enough, Hitler's passion for pointless bloodshed had its counterpart in Canaris's passion for pointless intrigue, as if the boyish thrill of being the devious masterspy—deceiving and entrapping everybody—had never left him. Even more weirdly, when everybody else was after Canaris's blood, it was Himmler of all people who stood by him because, to Himmler, Canaris personified the romance of espionage, which the SS leaders first found in the stories of the British secret service written by John Buchan.

Canaris was a Janus: he wanted power and influence and prestige, and as long as Hitler supplied them he played along; but he also thought Hitler would finish Germany off and so must be removed by a conspiracy of patriots. His thinking was usually not so black and white: a mood, a dream, would deflect him; an exotic journey would lull his mind; a chance to complicate something already complex lured him into baroque byways of intrigue for its own sake. Canaris the legendary masterspy who was also the pillar and patron of the German Resistance gives way to Canaris the stylish amateur who saved Jews and hired them but also came up with the idea that German Jews should wear a Star of David. He was less of, or with, the Resistance than within its rhetorical vicinity, lending an ear (or a desk drawer) to his more heartily motivated colleagues but sometimes not lifting a finger to help them when the Gestapo pulled them in. "I did it for show," he cried out during his trial in the laundry room at Flossenburg camp, and that is typical; he was such a hedonistic fatalist that he took no stand, other than self-interest, until someone forced one from him. Canaris had a pronounced sense of adventure, including the adventure of evil itself. Indeed, life with the Nazis struck Canaris as like getting involved with the gangsters in a competently written thriller. It sometimes seems that the whole Nazi bloodbath was a boyhood dream writ large and gone wrong, as befouled as the rug on which Canaris's two dachshunds gamboled in his office.

Canaris's associates, Oster and Dohnanyi, and then Canaris himself, begin to sway and duck, maneuver and slide, as the Gestapo tries to pick them off. Our documents, they protest, always mean the *opposite* of what they say; we're in espionage after all. We only *pretended* to play the *Fuehrer* false.

Canaris's intimate life was thin, but its external texture has its charms. His ancestors came from a silk-spinning village on Lake Como. As a boy he played with invisible inks and assumed false names; as a young naval officer he excelled by setting up a supply system for U-boats in the Mediterranean and floated through Spain, France, and Italy using a Chilean passport and the name Reed Rosas. His code names for espionage purposes were Kika and Guillermo. In command of a submarine, he efficiently mined Allied sea routes in 1916 and then confirmed his deviousness by thwarting justice at the court-martial of the officers involved in the murder of Rosa Luxemburg. Always accumulating informants and accomplices—kings, businessmen, diplomats, rogues, and financiers—Canaris came to a halt in 1931 when the German press dug deep into the trial he'd rigged. Then he marked time until his appointment to Intelligence in 1934, as head.

He comes through a bit forlorn, with three bronze monkeys on his desk to symbolize "see all, hear all, say nothing." White-haired, ruddy-faced, five-feet, three-inches tall, speaking with a lisp and looking nattily frail, he was a pill-popping hypochondriac, forever phoning from enormous distances to check on the bowel movements of his dogs. He slept inordinately. One officer thought he resembled "the impresario of a worldwide music-hall agency." In fact, he played croquet with Heydrich of the SS, cooked saddle of wild boar *en croûte* for his guests, and had an Algerian butler named Mohammed. His picturesque side includes saluting a shepherd in Spain because "you can never tell if there's a senior officer underneath" and suggesting to a colleague that, after the war, the pair of them "open a little coffee shop in Piraeus harbor. I'll make the coffee and you can wait table."

OBER-GRUPPENFÜHRER ROLF STUNDT

If only there were some way of informing all those who make TV documentaries about the fate of the surviving Nazis such as myself. It was never true that I had eaten human brains with a silver spoon from the crushed-in top of a skull. The spoon was gold. Removed from one gratifying job as commander of a Waffen SS formation and stuck into a hospital for observation, suspected of cannibalism and other things, I was a plain chap with developed tastes. I would have been ideal for Battista's Cuba. The myth is that I disappeared in Brazil or Paraguay. The truth is that I hid in a big reference library in Louvain, where those who found me incorporated me into the collection, first tying me up on the floor of a quite large room that would have held, in stack, a hundred men or fifty cows, then slowly sealing me up in books. First they built a little coffin of them around me, and then they filled the room with them, retreating for coffee and sandwiches, then blocking in another area until there was no space left. The door that opened outward swung home upon me. They drilled holes and screwed it tight. I felt like a cask of amontillado. That was '45. They found me in '46, unopened and unread, mentioned briefly in one novel, not on my chest of course.

BECKETT IN THE FIELDS
ABOVE AVIGNON

When they settled in, their shoes were caked with thick, red dust. He signed the register, saying his birthplace was Dublin, England, his address the Hotel Escoffier in this very same Roussillon. Lies. His home was in his head and only the French would not know the whereabouts of Dublin. Poor, battered place open to the winds, and all days alike. Loud Miss Beamish chanted Shakespeare to drown out the racket of her cats and dogs. You would no more come here to be inspired, he grumbled, than you would stand in a *pissoir* to read Spinoza.

He worked for wine and cheese, for Bonnelly at first. He babysat mothers. He had always been a great bedside-sitter to old women. He had the manner, he said.

Then he worked for Aude, chopping wood and slaving in the potato fields, a truly Irish lumberjack. Logs and spuds. Were there a book of the Bible, he said, devoted to those days, it would surely be called *Neuteronomy*. His daily round was one of work, chess, radio, coughs, and boils, and he was always having to sit or lie still in the small hours lest he wake the whole hotel. He had to fit in, as if he knew how. So he ended up in a small derelict house where he kept a tame but big geranium on the tiny balcony outside the bedroom window, maneuvering it into the sun by tugging a string. He could devote whole days to that: his tropical sinecure, he called it.

He slept all day, if he could, and as much of the night as he could bear to. And Watt was with him, he of the red thatch and long cylindrical green overcoat, the boot on one foot, the shoe on the other, his gull-like eyes overlooking everything. There they sat, goggling, two graduates of the same asylum, the place where they were supposed to feel inviolable. Giggling as the rats ran up and down their trews, happier still when the milk churns clanged, mornings, and later when the mailman spun by, whistling *The Roses Are Blooming in Picardy*. Ay, but were they blooming in the hills above Avignon, *here?* They eyed the distant pearly mansion where God had come to rest and Watt once worked as a servant. Mentally both he and Watt were always chasing ambulances.

And he still played at war, even in the thick of the heat of composition. He put the dynamite next to the geranium lest Watt butter it and devour it, lest it blow up the little doomed house. Some of the *Maquis* led by Monsieur Char the poet killed some Germans come to investigate the bale of tobacco dropped by parachute (it was like the top of the morning falling, Sam said), but nothing happened. They went away. Miss Beamish, he, and Watt then recognized that something final but of indeterminable purport had just taken place, in contrast with which Ireland was a hippodrome of joy.

Always an afterward, Sam said on receiving the *Croix de Guerre* for resisting. *Betrayed to the Germans,* his citation said, *he from 1943 was forced to live clandestinely and with great difficulty.* As ever. And ever after. He became a Frenchman so as to have no home to go to.

JOSEF GOEBBELS

That slut of an actress now rotting in a Polish pit, did she really say "Only in the case of Goebbels is the schlong bigger than the schlong who is the man"? How could that be? Magda, my wife, who has the simplest, most effective theories about everything, *mein Führer,* says that each time it makes a baby it shrinks by the thickness of a bluebottle's wing. We have half a dozen of them so far, all of whom we are one day going to have to poison with their bedtime milk (I just know it). I worry, *mein Führer,* how can the schlong be bigger than its wearer? And why should such a comparison ever come to mind, even that of a castoff, whining whore? I smell propaganda everywhere. Now, if Magda and I had spawned a thousand children, then just perhaps there would be sense in it. *Mein Führer,* I demand a public measurement, at your very own hands.

HERMANN GOERING, NUREMBERG, 1946

Fat men are the wisest dreamers. I always ate up sleep, on my back or side virtually weightless, and here in a cell on the lip of oblivion I still munch the same creamy finitudes, doting on sleep's huge maternal billow, lurching downward only to heave myself back among the living for a final hug. That wind chime from on high is the tinkle of a hundred medals airing. Inert I lie, half-swooning, lifting an eyelash, or rather the baby muscle that guides it, but the exertion kills me.

So, this is the final sleep. I have often wondered at the rough handling meted out by executioners and their ilk to the corpses they have only just made, crudely slinging the sack of potatoes onto the wheelbarrow, shoving the floppy leg into the waiting truck, and slamming it home behind the door. They do not even hose you down. Before the deed they affect a coarse civility of nods, head-lifts, tight lips, while the drums roll, the trap creaks, the dynamo whines. Then they belabor you about like a sewer made of cloth.

Well, you deathsheads, this is Hermann having his last little schlaf at his own bidding. Fat men make the best nodders-off. I will not wait for Keitel and the rest. To Keitel I said: "Never confess. Be a man. Shout an oath when they spring the trap. Curse them for scuttling the *Graf Spee*. Damn that little spirochete, Goebbels. Yell to hell with that *amateur* fat man, Churchill."

This is the sternest hemlock of them all, but it makes me purr just to think of the burly master sergeant from Utah coming to take me to the rope, and looking forward to his eggs and ham afterward, or whatever these bogeymen eat, and finding the big paunch has slipped ahead of them like a new-calved island, pink with poison, or a freshly barbered hog. Oh that I could have been wearing antlers at this moment, just for show.

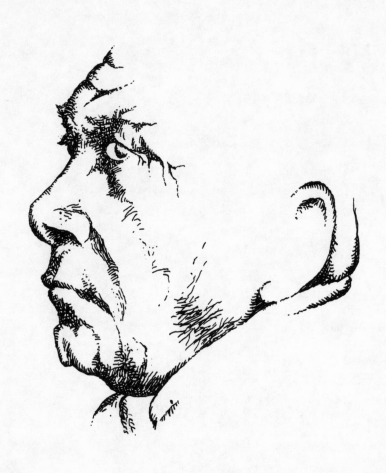

MARTIN BORMANN
(A Radiogram)

DEAREST MUMMY GIRL YOU AND THE CHILDREN MUST NEVER FALL INTO THE HANDS OF THESE WILD BEASTS IF THEY EVER REACH VIENNA GET OUT FAST I HAVE FOUND THE PERFECT HIDING PLACE IN THE TYROL YOU MY DEAREST GERDA ARE TO BECOME THE DIRECTOR OF A REFUGE FOR BOMBED-OUT CHILDREN NINE OF WHOM WILL BE OUR OWN I HAVE COMMANDEERED SIX OTHERS FROM THE NAZI PARTY KINDERGARTEN PUT BY PLENTY OF DRIED VEGETABLES AND HONEY YOU ALREADY HAVE THE MONEY AND GOLD AS WELL AS THE FÜHRER'S WATERCOLORS GO TO TYROL NOW CANCEL EVERYTHING GO NOW THE RUS-SIANS ARE ALREADY IN BERLIN BE A GOOD DIREC-TOR BARGAIN WITH ALL YOU HAVE WE WILL WIN THE NEXT ONE WAIT FOR THAT IF I HAD NOT BEEN NEEDED TO TAKE OVER FROM THAT SHIT-

SAUSAGE HESS NONE OF THIS WOULD HAVE HAPPENED IMAGINE THE FATHER OF NINE CHILDREN HAVING TO TAKE HIS OWN LIFE AS IF HE WERE SOME KIND OF BLOOD THIEF COPYCAT EVER M.

PAINTING (1946) BY FRANCIS BACON

W ho is *he* with shining ponderous jaw beneath bared teeth above which the face does not continue but vanishes into the wide-mouthed canopy of an open umbrella? He sports a yellow flower and a white collar, perhaps a nightclub bouncer installed on a railed-in podium flanked by fresh beeves, though the suet is white rather than yellow and may be fake. Above and behind him like a winged altar rears another skinned carcass, bovine no doubt, opened wide as a book, the ribs carmine and what seem furry catkins of bell ropes dangling from the roof, just touching the rent neck. The podium has an Axminster on it, and purple blinds have been drawn down from on high to enclose him in this chapel of meat, his black umbrella deployed against a deluge of blood. I think he is an overdeveloped bishop, too fat to be moved to the abattoir, and left here as a scarecrow to keep us from becoming believers, from offering ourselves up on his altar of flesh. This, ladies and gentlemen, is the bishop of our butcher's shop.

Unless that raised-back umbrella happens to be the black shell of some horrendous turtle got up like a choirboy, and his crystalline bowels (in which indecipherable figments float like vertebrae and gigantic lungs) are an igloo offered to us wolves.

WINSTON CHURCHILL IN MOROCCO

For Dave Madden of Lemitar Way

Why, out of office or moaning for rest, do I flee to Marrakesh
to paint under the burn of this unbalked sun, over which
electors have no sway? Lissom and free, making veils or laying
it on thick, the brush is too much rope for me. I come here
to daub at will, though, not copying Morocco but blowing
smoke rings of pigment until the next call to greatness. It
almost always comes.

The four things absent from my oils are tears, sweat, toil,
and blood, the four horsemen. This art of mine, so far from
my speeches, written out by chubby hand and made with
pudgy pausing, stays on the cuff. I sit for me, the image of
an artist: easel, stool, wide-brimmed fedora, smock, and cigar,
awaiting a Brighton photographer from pier or beach. Behold
the grand old soak at play, wishing that art were more like
bricklaying, at which I am good. It is more useful, more of

a *job*. Paint pliable does my ungifted bidding, like some undersecretary; it is like having, all your childhood days, a nurse named Everest, as I did, of lofty name and cozy lap. Eucalyptus breath.

One solace, Winny: Herr Hitler got his shadows wrong, as a Narzi would, doubtless from never laying bricks (another goldbricking plebeian) and too many eggs. I always wanted what others got without their getting mine. And when I did not, a fit of the Black Dog gnawed my heart. Would I give up even if I had everything?

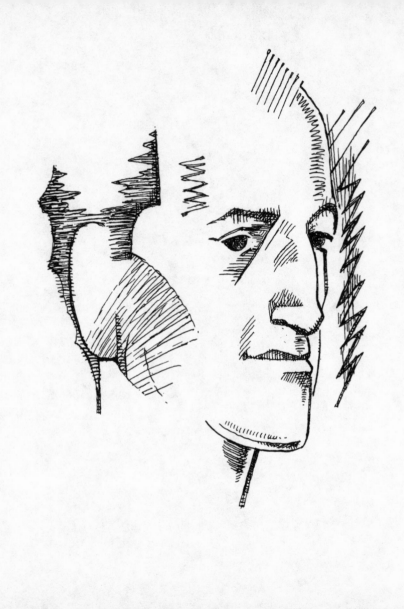

GEORGE GERSHWIN

I gotta get it, I'm gonna get it, I got it. Read it in the newspaper that Mister Paul, Mister Whiteman, Mister Paul Whiteman and I, I, I, I, we gonna do a piece together, a piece so different it will make the world stop and spin the other way, east-west. Well, Mister Whiteman and I, I, I, I, know nothing about this newsy little news item. We have no plans, though we do seem to have talked man-to-man some time or other. So I gotta take the train, see, I hear the rhythm of the rails—the word said *riddem*—and it is all there anyway, that long, dizzy ascent on the clarinet included. All I gotta do is write it down, syncop-syncop-ated. Cat-screech among the honored brownstones. An epileptic's gentleness with the balls of his feet. Three weeks only in the work, and it is a riot. Thank God for newspapers that have the brains to tell us what to do, to do, when we can't think of it. When in doubt as to where to go, even if destined to die young, go decide on a train, a train, and the train will tell you. And when you read in the newspaper that you died young, died young, you don't have to believe it, like that nice Mister O'Hara said. If you gotta, you gonna. If you gonna, then, then, you don't always gotta. Get it?

DUKE ELLINGTON

Aiming not to be too smooth, too downtown chic, when the wet-eyed band began to play, I made up music for a shaggy world full of mules and homeless dogs, dirty plates and airshaft shut-ins. Our moles had hairs growing out of them. We played the grapefruit rinds, the empty cans, the ghettos of ebony. Something cumbersome and roughcut was vital: tans, grunts, hiccups, washboards, and muted shrugs came with the indigo, the velvet. Our music lurched from rubato to showdown. We were cats yowling at the moon, not so slick or sharp as lumped together under shagbark. We growled our prayers into metal cones, making backstreet nocturnes that said nothing was flawless, not even the booksmart harmony of the old-time Greeks.

And yet, for all the hotsteps, and beats syncopated until there was nothing left but in-between, I was always yearning for that grander something: the symphony, the suite, making me, even if only for one evening, the lynx of *Nachtmusik,* his forte something contrapuntal to the point of mayhem, his weakness the old habit of, when the band cranked up, heading for the lowdown tune, when all the time there were battlements and esplanades, boulevards and plazas. I took the A-train once too often. In my wide pliable mouth there lurked a nightjar's blistered tongue.

COUNT BASIE

Unstrung by noise amid which hid a chime, a ring that sang, I saved one finger for the note that sealed a chorus. Black *embonpoint* hunched over a fairy's wink, I must have seemed dumber than ebony. *He plays so few notes,* they said, unable to spot a picky high-wire artist when one came along. Pink, link. Pinkety-plink.

I was Bill, I was William, I the count who eased his way in on there as of then, oh yair, somebody between lyric simpleton and chromatic oaf. I did not so much tickle ivories as caress them half to death, cunning linguist of the grand. The yachtsman's cap gave me tons of extra class.

Watch that ruby on his little finger, they said when I laid the keyboard open just a crack after all the rest had done and the melody was dying in the air in front of us, its energy new-gone. And then I did my county thing: never stretching a riff too far. I had a small and brassy band, a touch of cornball if you like, but with often enough the milky intimation of a world more delicate than the universe itself. Gossamer tux, bone-marrow wand. Fat man in a loose white suit embroidering his glee with big flourish of the pudgy wrist. Oh yair. The Count of Fin-esse. Pli-able. Dain-ty. What you always wanted but were too crude to say.

WOODY HERMAN

We were the loudest band of all. We never so much played music as assaulted it, and my clarinet was airier, flukier, than Benny's or Artie's. From me, the licorice came out like linguini in mourning.

All we ever wanted to do, while the accountants waited like vultures in mourning, was blow down a barn door, behind which we could hear the timeless jam of God's big band playing back to us.

If I ever looked a bit raffish, a touch shabby in my chic, it had to do with never knowing who did or did not belong in my band. Guys coming and going all the time. It could have been a hockey game.

We were a poem, though, a bazaar of mental kazoos. We let it happen. Those who came near and sang along with us, or dumbly danced, had no time to die.

I stole from Stravinsky, mainly for the brass, and he came up to me and said I steal too. I like the unison trumpet passage in "Caldonia." I'll write a concerto for you boys, and he called it *Ebony*. It flopped. He wasn't Brahms. We weren't angels. Half the band was asleep on dope. We got sick of playing "Woodchopper's Ball" every night of the year in places like Duncan, Arizona, dead all day and jam-packed at night just to hear us play. I had three Herds, but I was never a Napoleon. I didn't need to be. We were what one critic called *motoric*. They never split the herd.

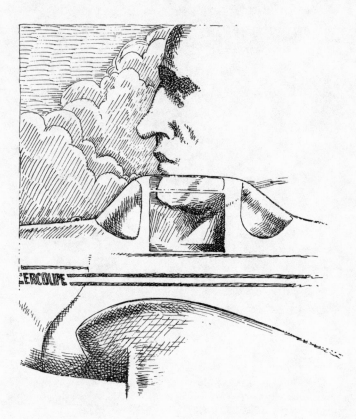

FRED E. WEICK

W ise Mr. Weick, designing an airplane for everyman, invented one that would not stall or spin. His Ercoupe, named prosaically after the Engineering Research Co., even appeared in Macy's department store: the first production plane with tricycle gear and steerable nosewheel. Not only that: you do not have to hold right rudder to allow for the propeller slipstream. The Ercoupe has a nosing-over moment too, which comes from the engine's being tilted five degrees downward as well as three to the right. In fact you fly and taxi an Ercoupe as if it were a car, pressing the footbrake when on land. It's a *coupe,* of course. People have died in it; it isn't that much of a velveeta toy. But, if you remember that it doesn't climb too well and lands funny, requiring touchdown partly sideways, you will do at least as well as the clergyman who, in cloud, found the wheel had come off in his hands and decided to pray, knowing he was in a craft that preferred ground to air, almost. Left to its own resources, the Ercoupe flew level and straight. Oh yes; the starting mechanism may drop into the bottom of the fuselage, and fuel from the gauge in front of the windscreen may obscure your view, but unless you happen to be a lummock through and through, you'll fly the thing with that odd, mellow sense of having cheated: like swimming without getting wet. As the old ad said, "You step into the plane, start the engine, drive down the runway, and take off." You also have to preflight it by shoving down on the tail section to let the buildup of water drain from the aft port. Flying the Ercoupe makes you eligible to receive *Coupe Capers,* the newsletter of the Ercoupe owners' club. It all sounds so cozy until you wonder how we know about the clergyman, who prayed and flew straight until he crashed, being unable to steer. He was overheard praying on his radio. What's needed, folks, is a plane that flies itself, against the day when those who use the Smith-Corona cartridge ribbon want to fly as well.

Buffs will tell you that Boeing trained 707 pilots in Ercoupes how to make crosswind landings because the 707 has low-hanging engine pods and so, like the Ercoupe, can't lower a wing into the wind in the usual way. More sybaritic buffs will read aloud the old brochures that whispered about the cockpit's gray and maroon motif, the richly carpeted floor, the buoyant foam rubber cushions, the two-way radio that enabled you to "converse" with airport control towers, and the draft-free ventilation system called air conditioning. *Ready. Set. Drive. If you have never flown, you have never known the pleasure to be derived from leaving the dusty earth for adventure in the clear, blue sky above. Worldwide distribution: Sanders Aviation, Inc., Riverdale, Maryland.* 1949.

Best of all, should your Ercoupe and Mr. Weick ever be in the same place, he will on request sign it for you as if it were a book.

EVA PERÓN

A theater poster from 1945 shows her face, but Eva Duarte's name appears only at the bottom of the cast list, perhaps because it was then easier to paint an arrow direct from her name to her face. The movie's title is *La Cabalgata del Circo,* a far cry from a forty-thousand-dollar annual bill from Paris couturiers, three-room storage space for hats and furs, and the Grand Peronist Medal, Extraordinary grade. In fact her salary rose from forty-five dollars a month, earned as a minor actress for Radio Belgrano, to seven-and-a-half thousand. Who said a raise is not inspiring? Even in furs, she was a shirtless one. In Spain she gave the Falange salute. In Italy, American GIs gave her wolf whistles; Switzerland greeted her with stones and overripe tomatoes, while Buckingham Palace refused to have her as a houseguest. Lincoln bombers and Meteor jet fighters overflew her funeral. A hospital director who failed to observe the official mourning period was dismissed for lack of respect. And her last wish was that, after her death, the poor should write to her. President Perón ordered all letters to be answered in her name and a special mailbox to be built in her monument.

She came from below, like the sun, like the sun her husband was. Yet, alas for all believers, her body lay in a secret grave in a Milan cemetery, under a nun's name, for sixteen years. When it was returned to Argentina, according to one exiled Argentinian novelist, it began to branch out underground, one arm going northwest through Córdoba to Tucumán, the other eastward past La Plata toward where the hulk of the *Graf Spee* lies on the ocean bottom, one leg out past Neuquén and Punta Arenas while the other grew parallel to the coast within the Falklands. It is not known how long this underground proliferation will last, but the letterbox in the mausoleum in Buenos Aires keeps filling with obscure, impertinent little notes from people called Famas and Cronopios asking why the soil rumbles and their pastures reek of burning celluloid.

COLETTE EN ROUTE

To convince a child or an animal is to weaken them. No one, certainly not Willy, who locked me up to make me work, would ever believe or let me think that what goes into a lunch basket lugged aboard a train is a collection of small beings. Grapes soft as oysters, minimally marching. Bread sprouting its beard. Cheese turning a pale green cheek like an albino monkey slipping into a vale of chlorophyll. Apples waiting to crack open like two clasped hands parting. The sliced meats are labia, the intact ox tongue a vaster tribute than they could withstand. The butter is a million molten daffodils. It is all of it too alive to be eaten, unless you believe, as I do, in mastication as lovemaking with the voiceless swains of life. As the train jerks and sways, we briefly make a living piece of ourselves this disinfected-smelling ham, this cozy banana exposed, this truffle nosed out from its universe by a pig. And the external world is no longer that, but deliciously blurred with us, mingled, melting, dissolving, not so much invited as raped. Before you travel with your food, you should sleep with it, and I always tuck a condemned pineapple into my bed-knickers before turning in. The discomfort becomes a fillip. Yet when I offer my fellow travelers this bounty, they flinch away, thinking I am going to poison them or lure them into the emptied basket, as if they rather than their heads would fit. It would be more inviting to fill the hamper with piglets, eels, ducklings, rabbits, pheasants, and ortolans, all venting their natural musical sounds. Add a sheaf of wheat, a churn full of milk. Limiting, but honest. Well, *mesdames et messieurs,* shall we take it from here? Produce the ax and knife. They too flee. One is condemned to savor things alone in the fastness of a mingled aroma so keen it could, if piped forward, drive the train.

What really drives them crazy is when I eat my jams with a knitting needle, making a slowcoach epicure out of the woman in the corner seat.

ROSALIND FRANKLIN

Almost a scold, she came to King's bearing upon her the attractive musk of some dark entanglement in Paris, to which her mind, while she nibbled ham sandwiches in a London park, often returned, as if only in Paris had she known how to live, having improvised it out of the air. Wise about coal, she now peered into the fibers of DNA, watching the X-rays diffract and trying to get photographs in which the universe came clean. She said she felt like an archaeologist peering into a long-sealed tomb, and she herself looked weary of time, a long-lost queen of basement donkeywork, rapt and aloof while all the others— Crick, Watson, Wilkins—dreamed of the Nobel and hastened toward it. "Let me know when you get going," Wilkins had told her, and she had answered "Why?" They must not call her Rosie or tell her that, seen at work, she seemed like someone praying to the ghost in the gene. She pored over Patterson calculations while the others worried about Chargaff ratios. For those boys, as she called them, it was only a game, whereas for her it was a prelude to the devout mapping of infinity, something that would go on without her when she applied herself to single-stranded RNA. Looking out at the London fog, she almost felt cozy, stared so hard at the Saint Andrew's cross shape of the electrons that it seemed to wobble and take off.

All of a sudden, the three of them had soared away from her, only Wilkins dawdling. They built a model of their mystery from freshly machined parts while, with eloquent firmness, she noted in her book that the structure of DNA was almost certainly a double helix. She blotted the page and closed the book, somehow unwilling to be more obvious than that. "I didn't see it," she told them later, but she had: her trumpet was quieter, that was all, and knowledge was its own reward, *hein?* Like love. They were gentlemen and scholars about it, putting her name along with theirs on the history-making paper. She died in 1958, five years after the discovery that brought them their Nobels in 1962; but there are no posthumous Nobels (one wonders why, or why there is no award for music or painting). It was as if, plucked away from them by cancer, she had saved herself from some vulgar follow-through, a mutual curtsey between King's College; London; and the Cavendish Laboratory, Cambridge. She had noted that the structure was a kind of *soixante-neuf* and so almost Parisian. God's frightful head had neared her lap and she had not flinched, the true dark lady of this cosmic sonnet, knowing the phosphates would still be on the outside even after the red giant of our sun had fried the planet she worked upon. Did she hear Doctor

Faustus howling in envy or the quiet, plummy hum from another batch of prime ministers?

VLADIMIR NABOKOV
IN CAYUGA HEIGHTS

A day of purest Arizona, this: dry, calm, and blue, tempting me to stroll abroad in the Arts quad of our famous university, where an open-necked shirt is formal enough if sheathed in a tweed jacket. When I first came here, I bought my clothing at the military surplus stores and have never felt closer to people than then. It was here I used to skulk behind the trees, then pounce upon passing (or failing) students to ask them if they knew what kind of tree it was. They never knew. I had almost no friends, American men having no gift for friendship (Swiss cuckoos are more cordial). Yet I was not looking for friendship today, or the names of trees, or even the dilatory afterbirth of the *Zeitgeist*, hovering like stratocirrus above Goldwin Smith; I was hunting no butterfly either, but the pensive silence for which universities are known. Amid which tenured geniuses think. All I could hear, however, was a barrage of uncoordinated drums and, raised in agony garbed as song, the unsorted voices of those who clearly cannot read. I was lone witness to the latest variant of Hottentot, who needs to bounce and twitch, deafened and barbarically exhorted, not to re-read *Madame Bovary* or the books of neglected Franz Hellens, but to swing out, sister, or something such, doubtless from a branch of some tree the simians cannot name. I had always wondered at the pigskin cult, but now I see the link to drums. The young come here to shove and shout. Or, rather, to watch others shove and shout. Is it for lack of a civil war that American universities are so physical? Their syllabi swell with boys' books, Hemingway and Conrad, for instance, and the subdominant hemispheres of almost all brains obey the nonstop music. I am glad that the bruited move to rename the Corners Community Shopping Center *Le Petit Coin Nabokov* failed because of the suddenly revealed erotic connotation involved. "Why," said one tweeded worthy, not having made love to a Lolita—*Loh-lee-ta*—"it would be the same as saying Cooch Corner. Imagine a bus stop called that." Had I been there I would have directed his etymological lobes to the derivation of Grove Street, in the Oxford of England and not that of the Mississippi windbag, couching the earlier word (if I may) in the headline phrase: Carnal Ukase, No Thoroughfare. Sea. Yew. En. Tee. (As Quilty might say.) 'Twas there, in the old days, Community Corners, et cetera, I bought my liquors, when I could afford. What a dismal privilege this Outre Tombe revenance has become. As if I am having my career all over again, I yearn for another, warmer lake, God (or royalties) permitting. I miss only the little ironing boards that swivel down. I miss the mucilage, the correction fluids, the misspelling of *pyjamas,* and the now-lost euphemism: comfort station. I even miss the petty Antarctica of the stomach as ice cubes go sledding endlessly through. I miss all the No-Tell Motels. The view from up here is ridiculous: one sees only the tops of closed books, gilt or tinted, mottled or plain. All Open Sesames have closed.

ZAZIE IN THE MÉTRO

Go, I tell them as I always did, and perform the anatomical impossibility. They weep jam. Lemon curd lines their drawers. They having a tuning fork up their asses. All of them, I mean: both the sexes. Give me, any day, a length of gleaming rail, or one electrified that I could slide my crease along. Monsieur Queneau, my creator, whom I myself call Coneau, was tickled to death when he turned me out of his imagination into the Métro, just to be uncouth and foulmouthed as a dockworker. Kiss my ass, I always had to say, or scrape the cheese off your old minaret, you filthy old sod. It was all right to see the look of hate and introverted shock—how the animals must have looked back up at God when He plopped them on the land.

I really wanted, though, to be a polite girl, bowing and scraping, with all the filth of my slang sealed within my mouth, and, drifting up from under my skirt, only the merest fume of crotch rot. I wanted to be a silent shocker, like an old caramel custard left under a leper's bed for ten years, long enough for a worm colony to have feuding heirs. My true maker was Pascal, who preached the horror of the silent spaces in the universe, not that of their immensity. I am the horrid, silent girl they will one day blast into outer space to pollute the silence with a grin like rancid cream. I have a date with M. Coneau there, just to pull faces. If you pull a face enough it will cease to speak and, slowly, ensheathe the entire body of its wearer. Take it from me.

HEITOR VILLA-LOBOS

If he was anyone other than himself, he was Bach, and then only while composing on graph paper, using little squares instead of notes. Only when he was that deliberate was he Bach.

"I claim to be *all myself*," he liked to say. Once he said, "What is folklore? *I* am folklore!" And he even claimed he was afraid of becoming the best composer in the world. He invented his own uniqueness and saw how far it had taken him, in spite of killjoys and uremia, right into his early seventies. He was a primitive modern, he was sure, fond of examining the webs that spiders rigged a hand's breadth from the window screen of the well-to-do, as if in homespun parody. Always, he preferred the webs to the screens as being more vital and complex. "They *radiate*," he chortled whenever outside, peering at the windows, "in wider and wider arcs, whereas the parallels in the screens will eventually have to meet."

Those were his great days, when his mind roamed, while he composed, through rundown mansions swathed in muslin decked with the sucked-dry abdomens of insects of all kinds.

One of his favorite serious pranks was to conduct choirs of children with two flags while he stood on the cabin roof of a tiny red and yellow railroad locomotive, its brass dome a stunning blob of light. No one had seen anything like him in the whole history of the world, and he knew this, and he was glad.

"*Ah!*" or "*chuf!*" the children sang untidily, but what a shaded "*ah!*" what a thrusting "*chuf!*" each time reducing him to tears because every child had a voice and every human was a child suppressed. Decade after decade, all of life teemed before him, and all he could think was how abundant the world was, how lush, how thick, how swollen, pouring and sprouting wherever he looked. What a privilege, he said, to be immersed in such a lavish show. How could it ever end?

One day, though, when he was seventy-two, his luscious plenty shrank all of a sudden to the image of a jungle bird with stained-glass wingspread, orchids for plumage, and a tusk for a beak: a private, wild emblem, brittle and shrunken, of which he could make nothing at all. Mother Nature halts, he told himself; she's bound to start up again. Surely she will not fail just because *I* am weakening?

There was a new, blank place in his head, where lurked all the things he sensed he could no longer recall. Under his quaking hand, the net of graph paper awaited his choice of a square, his inking it black or red; but now his fingers refused to move, and the usual hum failed to come into his throat.

He had reached a choric pause, he told himself; but pausing had never been part of his natural idiom, he who had been the maestro of onrush, as careless with his finished manuscripts as with money. Some enormous subtraction worked its will on him, erasing and numbing until he felt a mere vestige of whoever he had been. He felt like the human equivalent of a misquotation: gibberish on legs, but for the life of him he couldn't put his finger on the wrong word.

He tried groping back to his old self, there in his head somewhere, but it was like obsolete heraldry, unable to stir the present or quicken his gift.

He remembered how he had learned to play the violin, as a child, by holding it vertical, cello fashion. So that was *one* memory not gone. He remembered how his first composition had had a certain roundness, so he'd called it "Pancake." *Another* memory intact! Then he remembered how he had gone on to music shaped after the Paris or Manhattan skyline or the sawteeth of a mountain range: all on squared paper, in which an outline became the contour of a tune as naturally as grapes grew fat. Then, without warning, he couldn't remember what he'd remembered; he knew only there had been remembering.

Gone forever, and he didn't know it, were Negro chants gleaned in Barbados, where he'd once been stranded, trying in vain to reach New York, and the bombardine, a brass instrument rather like a tuba. Gone too were the valleys of the Amazon, the stark Matto Grosso, along with masks, jaguars, blowguns, totems, potions, interviewers, and the snazzy tunes in those restaurants where he'd first earned a living. He strained to recapture something, but all that came was a red flush.

I have no technique for now, he told himself. I'll wait, and afterward. . . . But afterward refused to come. An hour became a day stretched into a week. His skin dried and cooled. His eyes lapsed into pleasurable nonfocus. His head felt light and snuff-dry as balsawood, and he longed for a wind—ah, he remembered winds!—a green jungle wind, such as never was, to blow him into kingdom come. He wanted to be exhaled somehow into the noonday fug.

In fact, Villa-Lobos had discovered unseasonable time, the texture of in-between, when humans get the blues, cattle yammer, and birds of paradise lean sideways until they keel over. He was undergoing, without knowing it, what rituals are supposed to preclude. We camouflage time, not so much its passing as the sallow chasm between *tock* and *tick*. When the world is not a festival, it cannot be endured. He wept, self-searingly, with what remained of his mind, unable to use the lull, turn it into an event, or otherwise get through it.

What he felt had no formal structure; ennui, after all, was not a string quartet.

Nor was there a pulse, a heave, a bleat, to it. Ennui was not the jungle, either.

Nor was ennui quite the word, anyway, any more than it was the blues, or cafard, or tedium, or funk. The blight that swelled inside him, heedless and furry, was another form of life, like something extraplanetary found in Caipira, where the little train ran. Had he been able to make comparisons, he might have likened the hiatus to *Rudepoêma,* the almost unplayable piano piece he'd written for Artur Rubinstein. As it was, however, he weakened hour by hour and could only manage to accept the hiatus, much as he'd accepted the gift of his life—raw, as well as abrupt and slight—at eleven, when his father died.

This time, no other death could energize him, though. He was more deeply enmeshed in Mother Nature than ever. His cells were too far gone to wish to be free, and with what was left he dreamed he was being tweaked or strummed, but the only sound was the pale green squeak of the heart machine in the emergency ward. He groaned like a small animal.

It was November 1959, but winter only north of the other tropic. Yet his warmth had gone: the head-lava, the mulled aroma of his joy, and all he could hear was a pulse not his own, and far away, that of a zombie who could remember nobody's face and nobody's name, behind his oxygen mask, in a hospital under the sun, in Rio.

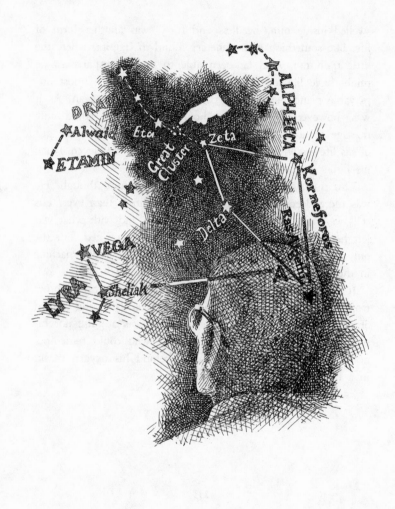

HENRY M. NEELY

In the sky, apple pie, at least in Henry M. Neely's *Primer for Star-Gazers*. When he looks at Cygnus, he sees a baseball game: *The batter has hit a fly to center. Albireo is running to get it and second-baseman Phi is also out after it. Shortstop Eta has run over to cover for Phi and leftfielder Vega is running in to back up third in case of trouble.* He not only wants you to get it, he wants you to say it right too: Eta, he says, is *Ate-a,* Phi is *fie* (rhymes with *pie* and *rye*), Vega is *veega,* and, oh yes, Albireo is *al-beer-ee-oh* (accent on *beer*). Not only that: in some of his constellation maps, a neat amputated hand appears with an inch of cuff on show, the forefinger dropped to indicate where, say, Orion is. For other textbooks you have to be as grownup as possible. You never get baseball and you may flounder for years when you wonder how to say Dschubba (*jub-a,* he says, rhyming it with *tub* and *rub*), though he adds that classicists disapprove of the name and that the government list of navigational stars ignores the classicists. The universe, when you look up at it, and so cramp the basilar arteries in the back of your neck, is so infantilizing anyway that Henry

M. Neely seems to be doing it right, treating us in its presence as the children we in fact are. Gone back into his beloved universe since 1963, is he getting close to one of those hands? Will he one day soon show up in one of the diagrams, complete with head and trunk and legs, reattached to his hand at last?

FRITZ ZWICKY, ASTRONOMER

Over the years I guess I wore those bastards down. I called them spherical bastards because they were bastards whichever way you looked at them, the diners at the smarty-pants Atheneum Caltech dining club. Down on the floor I'd land, challenging them all to one-arm pushups, and I never had a single taker. I got away with it, in a profession in which as always the plums go to the sleek, because I and I alone discovered supernovas. I also found the missing mass that holds the universe together. Among the great zooming minds, I am not such a little shit myself, even if in the final years they did shove me off down to the basements where the graduate students make love to their constipation. "Who the hell are you?" I'd yell at any of them. "I am Zwicky, the explosive, flat-faced, pale-eyed Bulgarian raised among the cuckoo clocks and the slotted cheeses. Tell them you have seen the great Zwicky at his most Bulgarian. I am the klutz who got it right." I never told them, though, my head was full of stars exploding long before I knew they could. With the gentle, timid, utterly neurotic cripple, Baade, I invented the word for them. Baade was a cretin, but others invented that word for him: not I. Baade used to go around asking "What if Zwicky goes mad? He's going to murder me." Baade and I sat at opposite ends of the dining table, but I never attacked. One evening I said, to them all, "We should launch a rocket to the moon to recover rocks for study." But all they said was "Aww, Fritz, leave the goddamn moon to the lovers." No vision, those fuckers. It was I who first thought of mixing explosive chemicals with the emulsions used in photography. Point the scope and the film would fry. You'd hear it. It was I who stuck a charge on the nose of an Aerobee rocket and fired a bit of metal off into deep space when the rocket reached its apogee. It was I who had a night assistant fire a rifle bullet straight past the Hale telescope and out the dome to knock a hole through the air to make the seeing better.

Those bastards in their smoking jackets, worrying about which fork to use. I am still at the little Schmidt in the cluster of carrasco oaks, and the universe I am still such a boor in is wilder than they think. And more boorish. I myself contain the missing mass. I am an asteroid named Zwicky. So is Baade. In the Main Belt. Will we never collide? Will we never arm-wrestle? I wait for all those bastards down there to come up here to be asteroids. Good evening, gentlemen. Now you are through, say hello to your favorite bull seal.

PAUL HINDEMITH

Dry powdery quirk of my work. All have noted talc in Hindemith. Wry pucker on dry metal, no wet at all although every now and then huge plateaux of emotion. Ever that way, able to go without mental water for a long time, omitting it in the identical way I have omitted S this far.

Small man on a hassock, I long to be near the ground; I draw my sustenance from it, I who infuriated the Nazis with an aria sung in a bathtub while atonality flashed like political lightning. Disgusting and obscene, raved Goebbels, befouled with musical impotence; *that* to *me* who had meddled with pianola, radio, brass bands, and the movies.

So to Turkey, then to Yale, and then Zurich. I made my music students study Pythagoras, angels, and saints, even the little-known marches for military band that Beethoven did in 1809. Ovations *grazioso* is what I did, but my heart lingers forever in my settings of Walt Whitman's "When Lilacs Last in the Dooryard Bloomed," when I thought I had caught the sound of the human when most straitened, hardly able to breathe or gasp: creaking, aching, crumbling, groping, tweaking. Tenderness on the rack and wrung out.

> My American tribute.
> Not functional music at all.
> No dust.
> Just the stench of pee-ed-in pants drying.

No ponderously monumental and commodious railroad stations. No mountains with mice in them. No ubiquitous Mr. Thomson kvetching.

Parade drum and army bugle only, beloved of Whitman. And lilac blooming perennial.

HANS A. BETHE

1

Star-shine, star-bright. Here I am on a train, big lumbering bear of a man with a head that might have been blown from glass, its tear shape tapering a long way behind me until the wispy tail trails off into nothingness. My elbows are melons, my feet are suitcases, my brain is an enormous beloved German swamp chafing like an immigrant at the blood-brain barrier.

I have been conferring. Behold an envelope for a bill I could have paid at home in Ithaca. So much for shaggy mind intent upon the stars. Now, Hans, you will have to doodle usefully. Well, the sun, then. How does it work? By breaking something down or building something up? It derives from nothing else, so it must have found a way of blowing its own trumpet. It keeps adding to itself. It keeps adding itself to itself, but without ever achieving a total.

It is obvious. Two hydrogens team up to find a third. Then the trio finds another trio. Four out of six make up a helium and the two remaining hydrogens like two drunks go off to start the whole thing all over again. I have just more or less figured out the sun. Now what? So much for the big blazing disk that almost blinded Newton. The sun makes a meal of itself. Is that how the brain behaves when it goes godlike? I wish the puzzle were not done or that Ithaca would never stop at this train.

Down to earth, I send my paper to *The Physical Review* but call it back so as to enter it in a contest for the best unpublished paper on energy production in stars. I win five hundred dollars, half of which I send to the Nazis so that they will release my mother's furniture when they let her emigrate from Germany, which they are willing to do. I do not tell them: By the way, you swine, I have just solved the problem of how the sun works. Can you use it? Can you use me? Now I publish my paper, having kept the secret of delectable starshine until Mama was safe.

2

He of the sun's inner workings, opposite me for dinner, rumpled and aloof with his Nobel Prize nowhere in sight. Then someone tells him about *Gala*, that novel of mine so kindly reviewed by scientists, in which the characters build a model of the Milky Way in their basement. A long, apparently unwowed silence ensues while, perhaps, he works out another sun, of a mythic kind. Then he almost grins, asking with tentative monstrosity, "A *working* model?"

CARL SAGAN

Face of a Guatemalan *poète maudit* with a flash of Cossack in his stare, a tall, slowly wheeling, big bird of prey with an eagle's beak above a turtleneck, he hovers bombarded in an asteroid belt of private snapshots that the bigtime cameras never see: lecturing in khaki shirt and fatigued-looking pants, the neck open, the sleeves rolled up; leaping into the surf off Cocoa Beach in yellow trunks whose rustle is that of sailcloth; spending an entire lecture fee at the University of Pennsylvania on models of pre-Columbian artifacts; tucking into his mother's potato pancakes; insisting that absence of evidence is not evidence of absence; talking daylong into a cassette recorder held like a razor (Occam's cordless); riding the *Mission to Mars* at Disney World with his youngest son; seizing the microphone at a scientific convention to get the discussion on track; wondering if one can speed-read Proust.

Doubtless the King Arthur of the spheres, he is also the discoverer of ATP, the prime energy source for tissue, and of the distinct but cryptic radio emissions sent out by quasars. He chilled my blood and my bones when he said that in five billion years humanity will be extinct or have evolved into some other form of being, and the continents of Earth will no longer be identifiable on a planet reduced to a charred cinder. Then I cheered up. Such devastation isn't aimed at us; it isn't aimed. No, a tiny virus who travels light will zap us, or a renegade fiber in the heart. Not even a snowball a mile across. Our grandeur will have long gone aboard the *Voyagers,* like dandelion fluff blown into abyssal dark, touring the vacuum, touting for business among, if any, the sentry cries of Who Goes There? Who? Who *were* you for so short a time?

RUDOLF
SCHWARZKOGLER

Ultimate artist, sonneteer of meat, you had one of the traditional short lives: with the vision accomplished, what remained to live for? Twenty-nine, a fuller complement of years than many, but with your body winnowed, shall we say. Did they call it body art back then, when the Viennese avant-garde laid you like a ripe and bloody egg on the doorstep of another Austrian butcher, who set up shop before 1940? With a photographer incessantly beside you to record that slow reduction of yourself inch by inch, you at last set to work upon your own penis, doing to yourself what Hitler liked to do to others (like that film of hanged conspirators he had *his* cameramen make). One is tempted to come up with the opposite of excess and erection, just for you: incess and derection? Will they do? You go into history as a mummy swathed in bandages and decorated with razor blades, which in your perverse iconography figure as Iron Crosses, although, if we are to be literal, more like the ordinary soldier's Wounded badge. The full panoply of your disfigurements had to wait until the 1972 exhibition called Documenta 5, in Kassel, where you triumphed, making the whole world wonder about your final paradox: at what point was there too little left to lop something further off? If only you had begun earlier, as a child, still growing, there would have been a true counterpoint of growth and loss, the young flesh growing almost faster than you cut it off. If only you had had something to say, a notion to apply your Occam's razor to, you would have infested our minds rather than sliced yourself in our dreams. But perhaps you said something after all: your scabby, mottled image is that of the millions dismembered by the wars, the young men smelling bad in canopies of lint and bandage, as if, indeed, you were a chapel of paring, a depot of mutilation, the mopped-up destiny toward which we hope only a few more million will have to go before the great age of body-awe begins. If you became the patron saint of minimalists, it is only because they did not start with enough, whereas when you took a little of yourself away, from yourself, you were doing it to all of us, beseeching us to stick together or else.

IRENE PAPAS AS HELEN
OF TROY

Call this Helen's douche. In Michael Cacoyannis's film version of *Trojan Women,* Irene Papas all too briefly plays Helen, whom we first see as a prisoner. The Trojan women are frantic with thirst, having seen Helen's guard backheel a pan of water to her beneath the bottom plank of the otherwise stone shack in which she is being held. Between the horizontal planks we see Helen first snatch the pan, then shuck her robe, and stand in it. Now she squats and appears to sluice her face, her hair, her shoulders, then the rest of her body. Although some of the water splashed out when she tugged the pan toward her, there is enough left in which to cleanse herself. She remains at the squat until a fusillade of stones from the Trojan women makes her retreat to the rear of the shack. Perhaps, as they see her (not as clearly as we ourselves do from our seats), she seems to be doing something lewder. Certainly she is getting ready to make her entrance, and apparently she has her finery with her, because when she emerges she is resplendent. When she says "Menelaus" to her vengeful husband, she does it in a purring contralto pillow tone, from the very center of a woman delighted still to be in heat. Papas does it with sleek carnality, driving the wronged Menelaus out of his mind all over again. Off he goes with her, raving about "a vile death for a vile woman," but we scarcely believe him.

Cacoyannis resumes all her shameless history in that one-word greeting, so brash and thoughtless. The sluicing scene is so powerful because no one says anything; all you hear is the trickle of water as Helen splashes herself, and you imagine the water in the pan beginning to cloud up while the thirsty women wait outside. It's almost akin to quotation from a brothel scene in which the man washes himself at some discreetly placed basin, except that this is a woman doing it, ill-screened from an audience of women standing behind the husband she has notoriously cuckolded. It is foreplay to yet another insult. Everything she's done wrong, Helen claims, is the fault of Aphrodite. Maybe so. Whether or not a woman watching this scene becomes thirsty, a male becomes a voyeur, another guard, another Menelaus; our first view of Helen is of brown eyes in their oval slits looking through a gap between two planks. We end up going into some privacy beyond the original text and the scene, not in order to comprehend it better but, rather, to flesh out its hints at almost unspeakable primitivism. We live in the age of the mini-Helen, which measures enough beauty to launch not a thousand ships, but one only.

NIXON IN CHINA

Here in the library, one can tinkle the ivories ad lib, cracking a smile at the chinks in between. It is good to get away from them. In their old, naïve way they are too sly for the likes of me. The two of them love to hear a foxtrot, and when she breaks into a dance, does the actual step, he restrains himself but looks quite horny. They belong in an opium parlor, both of them. But they have that oily skin and you always know they are doing their damndest to screw you out of something. Thank the Lord for a wily old negotiator like me, heart of Irish oak, most of all when they get this tong war look and you get dizzy looking into their hardly open eyes, as if you were falling backward off the Great Wall into the eye of the tiger. Dizzy, sweaty, that's how I get when they start to stare me down, and, wouldn't you believe it, I start to fumble and look sideways as if I am not who I am, plenipotentiary of decency. Of the power that came my way, let it never be said I wasted it, but without getting too formal, too much of a man in the golden chair, too unhusbandly, unfathering. This is a real country, even if you have to say it behind your hand, whereas ours, well ours is a bit of an easy mark especially for young crazies. I like to think a country keeps its rear end tight, all apucker, like this China. Does them good to see a turned-up nose like mine, but they don't go running all over the place to change the Chinese nose. No, sir, you could bomb pretty well any species of slants into submission, but you could never bomb them into changing their noses, their eyes, their ways with children's feet. A virtuous man needs something to fight against. That's why there is evil. Always another war to win out here.

That is why we have dragons.

That is why their women, from Madame Mao on down, have these twatlike slits in their dresses, to make you half believe that what should be between their gams has slid around their thighs and is ready there for servicing, like a wound from that ritual of the thousand cuts. I have not studied Chinery for nothing.

Never mind how closemouthed they are, there is always a way in, past the silks and the red-faced lions, past the gingerbreadmen soldiers and the plump sentries with their fur hats and their dreadfully kept nails. How come the country that gave us gunpowder and spaghetti needs a few thousand manicurists?

I am summoned. Mister President has been away far too long just to have washed his hands. Back I go to the foul and febrile element I work in: the vice of others, their vile buyability. As Pat says, the men in the suits have no suits. Here is a yellow peril that needs a good tailor too. See the supple bend of my threads as I move. Watch this old fox trot, watch me make these madams drool.

PELÉ

I do not look where I am going, not so long as others do it for me. I am that holy rubber eel, the missing link who shoots to kill and cries out *Love, Love, Love.* To read my mind you have to catch my body first. I make full use of the void between chin and kneecap, and you do not. I live off it, even when I am upside down.

My fame, they say, is the trigonometry of feint, then a ball struck curving by the first and only Brazilian atomic foot cannon. I do comets without tails. I am a black fluid with a volcanic alias. You cannot find me with anything in my possession. I loll at the horizon, *belo horizonte,* waiting to head the ball into play. I am Brasil's whispered S, and when I uncoil I am no longer human or Brasilian. I am the wind, the wave, the crown prince of skywriting. Gather up my dust.

Pay-lay, they cry, a hundred thousand at each adoration. *Pay-lay,* Pele cries back with tears of trembling awe. Now pass the sun to me, between their legs, behind their backs, without seeming to do anything at all, and watch me cage it in the net.

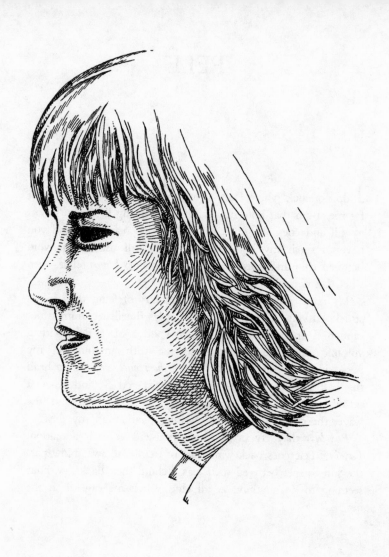

CHRIS EVERT

Taut and tight-lipped mistress of the baseline, she is the all-American golden girl become the champion of monotony. When she smiles, nets snap and tumble. When she quotes literature, entire audiences run screaming to the sea. Always photographed when perspiring, when her eyes have that glaze of someone wandering in the Kalahari for days. There is surely a being within all these exemplary strokes: the tennis equivalent (or match) of the Chinese water torture. Somewhere, in a distant galaxy called Florida, she beat a ball against a wall a thousand times a day and has a peculiar response to white or yellow lines. Mothered into linearity, she would perhaps, given choice, have been less automatic, a more boisterous, chuckling showoff. Her tennis almost brought back those other strict, weird sisters—Clotho, Lachesis, Atropos—into popular speech. When she mellowed, she became a player.

MARIAN McPARTLAND

You come to know her voice better than her piano playing,
with its opera singer's mellow crackle as if the cords are saying
not again when she hovers between a gurgle and a giggle,
interviewing, interviewing. Then she coaxes the well-rehearsed
guest into playing some popular number: "You've gotta do
that one. You're on the right and I'm on the left." Then the
guest asks her to do one, and, just as rehearsed, she says,
"Well, I'll try it and see what happens." Radio's her *boîte*.
She loves the old days, she loves any days, she comes across
as nifty, courteous, and, with that occasional mandarin hesitancy
of hers, a bit unaccustomed to speaking for a living. To one
guest, himself a radio host, she explains that she is the last of
the cottage industries ("I had Halcyon, you know"). Her
carefully cultivated dodder puts you in her debt at once because
you feel that, instead of being wholly within her own compass,
she is being stretched somewhat, and your ear wants to cross
the great divide of ether to save her, with a word, a quick
chord. Her tone is the affable-elegiac and behind her you can
divine the full percussion corps of long-gone piano players

aching to be on her right or left just so long as she goes on talking to them until she says to her listeners toward the end, "Now we're going to get into it a little bit." And the full, strict daintiness of her ways comes out over the piano as it spreads out under her tap.

EVONNE GOOLAGONG

Blackfella flair in every move, she runs as Marian McPartland, pianist, talks, with an almost stuttery litheness. An element of throwaway, of candid Aussie *Well, fuckit,* it's *only a bleeding ball, yn't it?* She tours the court as if songlines were beneath her feet, guiding her between games or even during them to some inestimably luscious rapport with clay or grass. She comes from the hinterland of the underworld of the unknown continent, with a white-eyed flash and a jaunty, unpaid grin. She remains an emotional amateur, a grownup prodigy with poise. In her something ancient and weathered, as if struck by lightning and groomed by constant sun, conducts her to where she needs to smash or slice. The ball will always be at the intersections of lines she senses in her toes, as if the furry scalloped thing had opened out, in the hands of the neighborhood Cubist, and become a boomerang homing on her like a prayer to its intended wave front. She walks off the court back to her life like a sultry Dauphin in search of her favorite kangaroo, for whom she saves cigars. Listen to her name: a puddle with a chime in it. She is closer to her origins than we are. When you play against her, you have taken on whatever it was that hey-prestoed the biped from the crouch. *Goolwa* is Aboriginal for *elbow*.

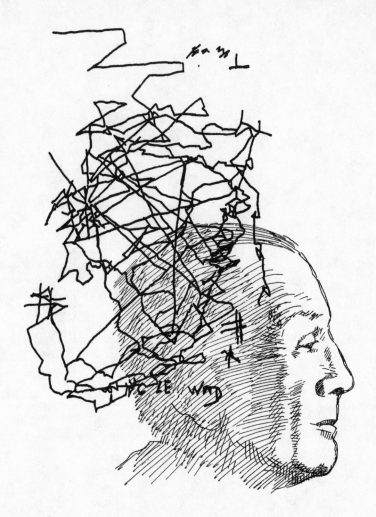

A BORGESIAN BEAST

Imaginary being, he called me, that silvery, dapper Argentine whose favorite word was *dim*. As if I were some volume in the infinite, darkling library of his mind. Why did he never call me what I truly am? I was never a white panther with black rosettes, the beast too blurred to be seen, too shy to look blind men in the eye. According to him, I looked down, too fierce to be seen at all. Only when I did would other beasts approach, and when they did (said my Argentine) I fell upon them and devoured them. Never. No, dearest folk, I could have been a rainshower chasing a white sheet, a burst of shellfire pitting a snowy plain. But I was not. I was never cinders in milk. I was a dalmatian, named for islands, and only a legally blind man could have seen my apparition in such black-and-white opposites: I was the beast made by the figure his shadows cut into his glare, I was the ghost his penumbra pocked with craters, I was the black night of the soul mended with balled-up white hankies. I was all imagery. I was a deposed chicken inspector dreaming of a panther who imagined a leopard in the act of devising a dog.

THE SHAH
OF IRAN

He has not used the streets of Teheran in many years; he goes to the airport for the last time by helicopter, a royal helix. One general, falling to the tarmac to kiss his feet, finds the former monarch lifting him back up just to kiss his hand. Like a dead mouse flung into orbit, he goes to a bolt-hole in the Bahamas, along with 368 pieces of baggage; but not for long. Next stop: Panama, guest of Torrijos, who tries to get Queen Farah into his bed while the Shah withers, a *chupon,* a sucked-out orange, squeezed by a dozen nations while the crab within him feeds on what is left. Who shall treat him? France or Panama? By the time his ghost fetches up in Egypt, he treasures most the chocolate box full of medals and decorations. Little had he thought, when the SAVAK were sewing up the lips of poets with wire in Teheran dungeons, it would come to this, or when he threw that party in Persepolis in 1971 to mark the 2,500th anniversary of the Persian Empire, cost $300 million dollars. He dies before rumor comes that his successors, madmen of a special stamp, have begun using the same poets as fuse-boxes, their mouths pressed firmly to the source of power.

IMELDA MARCOS

Miss *Manila calling.* She hears a dream, when it was wartime in the doghouse of the heart, although a garage is where she started, only nine, jammed in with Mama Remedios and the other kids, next to the fumey clapped-out car, whose metal was a foretaste of the corrugated iron prefab in Leyte.

In one painting, where an oily tropic sky walks the full moon out from under its epidermis like a tumor of shrapnel, she just touches his hand: the nail of her little finger taps his third knuckle, receiving the current. In the end, Manila's 400 accepted her, but never with the homesick fervor of the GIs to whom she crooned. Tried for Miss Manila. Sounds like an offense. Lost, having no money with which to win votes. So, as they say, she intervened personally with the mayor, and it was all right after that, apart from the weird games he liked to play with leeches. Then Ferdinand the Bull, the sawed-off nouveau riche living down a trial for murder, underpacked the rugs with so much moolah their heads rode ever nearer the ceilings. They were the only patients to whom doctors offered *quantity* of life. Retinue of 700 at the White House.

Fifty-seven, she competed for Miss Manila all over again, purring how contestant Aquino had no makeup, no manicure, whereas "Filipinos are for beauty. Filipinos who like beauty, love, and God are for Marcos." Could Cleopatra be a klutz? Never in all her lovely life did Miss Manila have a thousand breasts or six thousand feet, but only two knees, on which to blunder up the aisle all the way to the altar, as if the altar were another open bank.

FREYA STARK, TRAVELER

Alone in deserts for so long, I at last became a Dame, made so by a queen, but to American ears at last boosted from spinster to woman. Having boned up on Turkish, I was equipped to wander off over the rim of the world, but the Turkish helped only during massacres. Broke, I lodged with a shoemaker's family in Baghdad, city I adored, happy as a beetle mother and as plain. I had gone native, the other English said. Was it there I learned what spinsters do to cheer up? They buy a new hat, beneath which like melting cheese a new smile forms.

I was a naked female soul in love with barren places and the ruins that flowered in them, such as Ukhaidr. One might say the same of the Duchess of Windsor—her face the ruin, I mean, with heavenly clothes enfolding her. I wanted a baby Austin to run about in, after all those years of horse and camel, but it looked so—*dowdy* (having groped for the word, at least underline it in tribute). Tophole inside, I was told: not me, the Austin.

Only the things we say while walking matter.

One desert tribeswoman came and asked me if I had any medicine she could kill her husband with. I felt sorry I had none. I wept when I saw the bronze bust of Demeter. Oh, I felt, that every single woman could become that, even if she turned to salt first. Ozymandias in a corset.

Remember that I was named for a goddess of love and beauty, the rest of me bare and blunt. I am not in the *Britannica*, but my footprints are all over Arabia.

FELICIA MONTEALEGRE

Would you heed a deity who insisted on decorum and wouldn't let you off? In his Third, *The Kaddish,* at the last moment dedicated to the memory of a slaughtered Kennedy, the female voice addressing God in the *Din-Torah* cries, "Tin god! Your bargain is tin! It crumples in my hand!" As the liner says, "from Moses to the Hasidic sect, there is a deep personal intimacy which allows things to be said to God that are almost inconceivable in another religion." Just so. But it would not be the same, coming from any other female voice, for the speaker, Felicia Montealegre, happens to be Mrs. Bernstein, orating with rapt, almost histrionic intimacy as if not only the conductor-composer but the deity too were on stage with the Philharmonic. She flings her head back in spotlit orison. Her hands rise from the lectern like doves disturbed. He studies her deep and trancelike elocution as her literal enthusiasm mounts: Mrs. Bernstein is being possessed by a god against the will of the music. It is 1964. Some twenty years later, the same god has possessed the *Kaddish*'s speaker in a different and more final way, and the ghost of this recording is not JFK, but Ms. Montealegre. The composer retreats to his bed for six months, almost as if he were Elgar, and no one can bear to play Columbia KS-6605 again. It has become a palimpsest of grief amid which the unoffendable deity appears to have struck back.

ROY HARRIS

Yup: Grandpaw drove the pony express, he and Paw went off to Oklahoma, built them a cabin there with just an ax. We had a phonograph, a Edison, with those sigh-lindrical records, y' know. I read and read, Shakespeare and Greek philosophy. I ran my farm real good. I do most things well. Then I trucked butter and eggs to places off the beaten track. In California, that was. I went to Rochester and stayed five years, bust my spine, wrote a string quartet, stayed true to Bach. By 1935 a national poll had placed me first among American composers and an international one put me just behind César Franck. It had begun all right. During the blitz on London they chose a hundred works to be saved, and my *Third* was the only one by an American.

Well, iffen I was a cornball, I got to Cornell anyway, as composer-in-residence, just about self-taught by them sigh-lindrical records. I just wrote all the time, I was on earth to do it, and I raced a fast car whenever I could. Open-air music, mine, of the prairies. Bury me there or in the streets of Laredo. I excel at the passacaglia. Contrary to Virgil Thomson, I was never awarded by God or the U.S. of A. a monopolistic privilege of expressing our nation's deepest ideals and highest aspirations. I came right on the heels of César Franck, breathing down his neck. My pieces do not always begin alike. Boy, you sure lose buddies fast in this game. Old Virgil, he wrote right under my photo: "Roy Harris, in youth squarely a charmer, in middle age a business man, later prone to anger," but he did add "at all ages clearly a star," so it's okay, Virge, I ain't agoing to slug you now up here. Just you keep away from my beans and flapjacks, let me hear the clank and jingle of the old corral, the clap-clap sound of steaming hoss-flop, the pounded triangle that says Come and Get It. Should I have smoked a foot-long pipe like Ruggles or worn a dicky-bow like you and Aaron, with one of them boiled shirts?

Just you give me the strong silent sun and keep your Pulitzers to yourselves.

HANNA REITSCH, 1979

When they ask if there was anything I never found in life, I tell them, yes, *the thing that frightened me*. It was never there. So there is nothing momentous or that brave in a dying woman in a glider, setting yet another record over the punished-looking upper geology of the United States. In my day I flew rockets and jets. When the Führer gave me the Iron Cross in 1942, I told him it should be made of aluminum. An iron one should be pinned on you red-hot and then the metal put back into the war effort, leaving you with a permanent decoration in the flesh. You can tell I began as a flying missionary; I never lost that fanatic, plain-as-celery zeal. In the suicide squad in 1945, which flew to his bunker and stayed long enough there to watch him disintegrate along with his bourgeois Eva, I was a woman alone, as ever, even more alone than when flying a glider over the Alps or running that gliding school in Accra. I flew warplanes, but I never saw combat, alas, that artform engaged in by the very men who, having seen me fly over them, could not believe I was the same woman, the same pilot; an insane and unwholesome obsession with my private parts infected all of them. They could not wait to fondle what had shot over them on high, as if hypoxia were some aphrodisiac peculiar to me alone. Whereas I wanted these bully boys to clap me on the back as a comrade-in-arms, sharing a flag, a cause, they wanted a lotus blossom that had eaten wind.

DJUNA BARNES

If *inter*viewed, I would insist on being *viewed* beforehand, in a warm room full of purple sponges. I would be naked, supine, and the sponges would be squeezing or draining purple ink all over me. Only then would I consent, when the interviewer had bowed to the crumpled smile I sit upon, the smile that sits atop the closed parenthesis of my bowed-out legs. See how the little puckered mouth sits inside the wide one of my legs, both of which I have dried and daubed with red lipstick. A human might move through that *bouche de jambes* on the way to my other mouth or off home, right beneath my hams. I am not the lady I was.

Now I am kvetchy, touchy, curt. No this is not the interview, this is the complaint about interviewers. I no longer wish to be bothered, diddled, licked, loved. Not even to be flattered. It all comes back, like oysters repeating, but I do not feel like its proprietor. What was it that Joyce told me about Wilde? In the morning he studied the Restoration through a microscope and then repeated it through a telescope in the evening. By evening, the Restoration shows up better, like a cut-rate Pleiades on the dried-out chest of a dead and nutbrown nun. Well, I have seen Restorations aplenty, and there is nothing restorative about them. Had it been I, I would have used the telescope in the daytime, to distance things, and the microscope at night, to make them bigger when everything had been humbled and shrunken by the *congé* of one not wholly charismatic star. How could *I* be Oscar anyway? He could always, as men can, volunteer to be made into a eunuch, whose voice without overtones is so important to the church. But clitoridectomy, dear, is quite different, doing absolutely nothing for the voice. Twig it? There is nothing left to play with, whereas—dreams, dreams. I am a woman whose tragedy, like *Hamlet,* has been told from the viewpoint of the ghost.

Is *this* the interview, then? Has it begun? Why are we rehearsing the rehearsal? You have such faith in my longevity, in my very Evity. It was Joyce again, naked on his back with a full saucer of warm tea on his naked and very flat belly. "By the toime it's cool," he told me, "Oi'll have the notion I want." I thought a better trick than getting the notion was to lift the saucer off one's belly without spilling a drop. Should it not have been perched, instead, on what was lower down: the impartial addenda of foliage? A saucer not to be upset in any way, of good sweet thick Indian called Morning Thunder, dark as nun's chest.

Joyce was a friend, Nora too. We talked of death, rats, horses, languages, climates, the sea. To me he looked like a half-blind pilot in goggles, both eyes in glass cockpits, the blind eye wide open, the good eye shut, but on his face a look of preposterously benighted accuracy. A compass steered his face, making him give that little jeer now and then, lifting and rounding his upper lip. His children were large, always growing taller so as to reach up and touch with their head-tops the red magic carpet of hair that Nora cruised beneath, *spushally* (as she said it) *whun* there was wind. They could all have flown to China on it. He drank his cool thin wine through cool thin lips that seemed to narrow into a pencil line and then retract altogether into his head. Heavily thin, he: how the portly might look if regularly squassated by the silly Inquisition.

WILLIAM EMPSON

"Slops," this poet and critic answered when asked what food he preferred, and he cooled his soup by squirting it back into his plate as if trying to cool his whistle. In the dead of winter he walked through slush and snow in ordinary shoes, from his apartment to his office, about a mile; so I found and, at the kneel, fitted to him a pair of rubber overshoes, which he never afterwards seemed to remove. Before succumbing to his daily monsoon of cognac, he spoke in lively fashion of Newton, China, and Yorkshire, usually in that order, and then students used to creep up on him and gently spin him around in his office chair as if he were an astronaut being tested for vertigo. He never woke up during these rotations. He went back at night to a place full of rotting oranges, used tissues, and odd socks. *Don't you know who he is?* his South African wife kept saying. She was the eighth type of ambiguity. Off he set, to visit Wallace Stevens, who had died twenty years earlier, and back he came, saying with his best military-colonel-cum-Tory look, "We are none of us getting younger." If he made the journey, who knows what he found at the other end. A palm, perhaps. He wrote the best poem in the world about a woman putting on her nylons. He once, for some minutes, watched my neighbor's door lamp through my telescope, thinking it Mars.

HOWARD HANSON

A man born in Wahoo, Nebraska, deserves all he gets, especially when Wahoo sports a sign that reads "Wahoo, Birthplace of Howard Hanson," best known to motorists as the man who wrote the music for *Alien:* big romantic forever to be associated with the spectacle of a well-set-up blond astronaut undressing in a small space vehicle under the eyes of a horny monster that drips acid. Did you know that was my so-called Romantic Symphony? Did anyone stay after the movie to read the credit crawl and let out a grand yippee for Howard, who had finally made it? After that movie, I linked my Second with something else: my *Lament for Beowulf,* almost a lament for Howard, just to distance myself from the thought of background music and a girl called Sigourney (whose name sounds like an African capital). I picture the vast burial mound by the sea, on which the funeral pyre of the eighth-century hero is built. They build a great big beacon and put the trophies on it. The women go on howling but they do not undress. Now the young warriors surround the bier and tell how dead Beowulf slaughtered the monster Grendel. That was the link. They thought they had Grendel in the spaceship all along, as if the ship were a haunted castle and the monster were behaving according to the translation by Morris and Wyatt. I wrote some of it among Scottish mists, my mind on Sweden, redwoods, and the broad prairies of Nebraska. I will take some stopping now.

KAREL HUSA

In his mind, uppermost, a Czech village, Lidice, razed by Heidrich's Nazis; in mine, a French one, Oradour, treated likewise. He writes a ballet about Troy, conquered and shriveling to ash; I write a novel and anonymize the town but see it as a Lidice in part. Years later, at Cornell, I have taken across the grass and clay between Goldwin Smith and Lincoln Hall the Rat Man's little book and, as if by magic, a square wafer in Christmassy paper has arrived at Goldwin Smith. "It could be music," says one of those waiting to watch me unwrap it. "Oh, it is, it must be," says another, "it's that shape." It is as if the music of his Trojan women has flowed back and forth over my pages, all forty-three minutes five seconds of it, in obsessed reciprocity. About the nastiness of the world you have to remind yourself again and again; we build so fast upon every shred of cheer. We recite the horrors to see if, in some laceratingly forlorn way, they appeal to us. The world is crueler than we can believe it is. Those who bear witness are not waiting for the horrors to unhappen. They are saying, perhaps to others, from Alpha Centauri, We are made of this. Beware.

Within a year of *Troades*, Euripides was a citizen no more. We are just fumbling for his hand two thousand years ago.

And then, in 1990, folded close like those seeds that mimic a closed umbrella and the medical shunt that lurks in a vessel of blood, Euripides's hand gropes toward the light and signals from Prague that Husa shall come conduct his *Music for Prague* for the first time in his native land. He goes, equipped with mutes for trumpets and trombones since these are in short supply in and around Smetana Hall. He gives the old V-sign to the audience, recalling how in his cottage on Cayuga Lake he first heard about the tanks, in 1968. Citizen of music, he becomes a Czech all over again, recognizing that the mutes, delivered in any year other than this, would have been less useful than symbolic.

THOMAS BERNHARD

The polite calculating ones will almost always outlive the likes of him, who died hating Austria so much that he forbade publication or performance of his works in Austria for the duration of copyright. In its sordid postwar clinics, Austria had killed his mother and his grandfather. In a sense, his whole life was an example of what Gottfried Benn called the domestic form of emigration: going without going, annulling oneself without getting a permit, putting up the shutters before the *Krystallnacht* begins. *Non serviam* we call it. Was it all really like having to ride that healthy-looking bicycle around and around in the whitewashed basement, ideal for use as an execution cellar? Only the girder and the meathooks are missing. You can see how clammy he looks, his eyes on the ground that is already dizzying him. He is an underground man riding himself. Perhaps if he had painted the tires with white paint, he would have seen the almost infinite criss-cross convolvulus of his circlings on the dark floor. Or perhaps it is not a cellar at all but, somehow, the corner of a building, or of two, and he is just going around the corner to pick up the newspaper.

Unlikely. Stockhausen locked himself up in the house for seven days with only water, and Bernhard belongs in the same school of punished virtuosity: cradle or bicycle the rack, disease and death the final alms-giving. He lived for as long as he could stand it in the country that lists more givable decorations than any other and still refers to Jews as gas chamber-shirkers. An American literary organization rescinded his invitation to New York; he was not a collegial man. He pissed black into the Danube to see if they would drink it, and they did.

MARLENE DIETRICH

Sternberg made me, as a certain poet might have put it. When I sit, I like to feel I hear a slither of limb on limb, two gliding tenderloins, whereas from those others, the "You will, Oscar" mediocrities, you hear only the sullen chafe of poor-quality sandpaper. I was always grist for the mill of a towering genius; I was a genius of malleability, had the rest of them only known. Man cries out for Marlene as Marlene cries out for form. *Sinn und Form,* folks. What a shame the Jesuits never had a studio of their own. A body made in perfect proportion does not have to be nailed to a cross to be savored, nor does a good mind have to show itself off in the company of peacock brains. Where do they breed the Garys, the Waynes, the Stewarts? They see the well-honed limbs and yearn to beat themselves to death in the fragrant abyss above the join. When I am older, I will write elegies for Cocteau, Malraux, Tynan, Ernest, and Jean, and, when I am gone, the whole world will feel my sorcery plucking at them still, as if I were Paris and they were Burbank. What they do not know, but could easily find out (even if they did not believe it), is that, to create the sucked-in facial look uniquely mine, I early on had my upper-rear molars removed. Two dimples from the dentist, *nicht Wahr?*

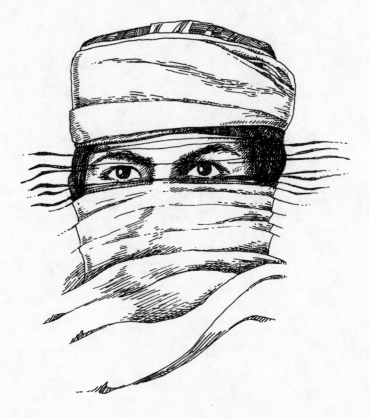

THE BABA OF RAI-BOUBA

As a child, he had always known that wearing it, as one day he would have to, was going to hurt him, the sharp upper edge cutting into the bridge of his nose, the just as sharp lower one cutting his nose only an inch lower down. Cloth, of course, but bandage-tight, making him a new version of the Man in the Iron Mask, with his black eyes visible in the slit to anyone rash enough to look. It was the kind of rectangular slot from which a death ray might leap forth, through a vizor gap in a helmet made of steel encasing lethal tubes and paralyzing voltage. As if he were not human at all. That was what worried him: at some point, he knew, he was going to change his appearance, become superhuman, and expect never to be looked at again. King, *Baba* to all, he was going to be sealed away into a heaving privacy behind yards and yards of pale blue cloth, allowed to speak with an aide only: worshipped, fawned upon, but never again (he shrank from the word) enjoyed.

Even his father was as remote as a sentry, a tall and burly presence who, if he perspired under that roasting sun, wet his inmost winding cloth with it and never flinched. Scald Ibis, as the son was called, kept on hoping he was going to have a different life from his father: an heir who did not inherit; but inherit he did, after his father's first seizure, although by then he had been away to foreign lands, had sampled the porridge and the hazing of Eton followed immediately by the laid-back rather previous intensity of King's College, Cambridge, where he lived for three years, a black man apart, boning up on economics and European history. How odd, he thought again and again, that we prepare our young kings for a life of virtual entombment by sending them to fancy schools full of extroverts. Surely they should wall us up when we reach the age of ten, and then we would do better. It was hard to tell how well his father did; his father never said anything, even through his human mouthpiece, and conducted his life through signs. Ideal for a taciturn man, this kingly vocation was the last thing Scald Ibis wanted. He had even asked, receiving only the answer that, if he were to try to abdicate, he could be found floating in Lake Chad. Or most of him would. Inheriting was part of nature, and nature did not change.

So here he was, not so much ascending the throne (an ornate and confining chair in which he actually sat) as whirling himself into the pale blue cloth of state, a young king almost seven feet tall. He could have anything else, and he did: his library had more books in it than his harem did women, and his arsenal of toys was full of chemistry sets, erector sets, and miniature civilizations from all over the earth with everything cast in lead and exquisitely painted. Turks, Eskimos, Kaffirs, Mohawks, and Blackfellas: he had the lot and sometimes melted them down in one big pot, pretending he was creating a second America. Yet even his talking toys said nothing to him, neither the tin parrots nor the windup whales, and the big white hangar in which he kept his toys repelled him, at first sight a sparkling panorama of all possible human appearances, but after a minute or two's thought a dead fort. "Birmingham" he called this hangar, vaguely recalling the city of cheap metal goods, and wishing he could have just a few robots for company. No, that was not quite it: he wanted to go out and about and talk with people instead of remaining this demon of holy rectitude, whom his people showered with gifts he had imported for them to give him. He wondered at the reflexive nature of kingship, that never left homage to chance, and wondered too if gods were the same. A big dish brought him channels from worldwide television. His supply of serious music was endless. His queen could quote Baudelaire but said nothing directly to him, even in the small hours of morning when he forced her hardest, to make her groan or plead. He lived in a desert of telescopes, orchids, and music boxes while an Oxford-educated prime minister ran the country and Rai Bouba, true to form, obeyed, paying its taxes on time and living in his prodigious shadow.

One thing his subjects always envied: when he went out of the country, which was not often, two retainers walked before him always, dropping from a black velvet sack enough soil for each foot, so that he was always walking on the land of home. In this fashion he might, so to speak, have walked to Alpha Centauri and set foot there without so much as making contact with foreign dirt. Those who bore the sacks of soil for him became in time deformed, bent double, but that only gave them an extra touch of humility when, back at court, they felt him slip over their heads the pale blue ribbon of the country's highest order: Sash of the Earth-bearer, which hung and swayed in the space beneath their horizontal necks. They went around like honored coalmen, bent forward for a beheading that never came.

MIZUSHIMA

We have all heard about the Japanese soldier who for years did not know the war had ended and lived on in the jungle, oblivious atavist, in poorer and poorer health until discovery, somewhat akin to the Polish novelist, Gombrowicz, who once upon a time set off from Gdynia on a pleasure cruise to Argentina and stayed there a quarter of a century. Precursors, these. Now I have seen *The Burmese Harp,* another image haunts and teases me: of a Japanese soldier, yes another, who marches in postwar Burma from the site of one atrocity to another, mourning the dead and communicating with his fellow-soldiers, now prisoners of war or peace, by means of carefully tutored parrots fresh-caught in the jungle. When I "teach" next, I will know how to do it.

OLIVIER MESSIAEN

He roosts now in a trellis of devout *glissandos,* sometimes larding his music with what sound like themes from an old Hollywood epic played in the wrong key; but in 1940, on the run from the Nazis, trudging from Verdun to Nancy, with his little haversack of scores (Bach to Berg), he was captured, stuck into Stalag VIIIA at Görlitz, where, having found a cellist, a violinist, and a clarinettist among his fellow prisoners, he composed a short trio for them to play in the washrooms, then, with himself on piano, a full-scale chamber work: *Quartet for the End of Time.* Was this when something rapturously corny began in him?

Hunger made him dream of colors, the colors of sounds, and one morning he saw the northern lights, those green and violet drapes "folding and unfolding, twisting and turning in the heavens." No beds in that camp: the prisoners slept in big wooden drawers, like bolts of linen, marooned in a wilderness of Silesian snow. Drab and ashen as they were, he and the others were a rainbow in that landscape, couched in the bottom of its abyss: Jean Le Boulaire, Henri Akoka, Etienne Pasquier, and almost five thousand others, hearing Messiaen's music abolish time and space as, at daybreak, a blackbird or nightingale broke the silence in its own way, part of what it had not been intended to join. It became the clarinet as Messiaen, at the broken-down upright piano, led them in his ovation to Saint John's mighty angel of the apocalypse, to whom or which the score is inscribed.

All you have to do, in order to release yourself from that snowbound camp, in the dead of winter, deep in the broken heart of war, asleep in a wooden drawer while dreaming of green and violet rainbows that are not food, is to close your eyes and become one of the five thousand far from music lovers whom he fed that January morning in 1941: highbrow music not that far, at times, from Massenet and Glenn Miller, Korngold and Tiomkin. Like a crystal handshake in the igloo of pain.

Somehow I am not surprised to learn that White Cliffs in Utah has been renamed Mount Messiaen. It is as if a man, having climbed that high, stepping on thin air, needs a mountain underneath him to make him look normal.

ERIC THE ACE

Oh he had one, but it was not his heart we heard when Flight Lieutenant Eric Plumtree thundered over the village he and we were born in: rooftop height, banking to make his letters and numbers easy to read. Overendowed with engine, a Rolls-Royce that thrummed a cantata of oil and muscle, his Spitfire was a boomerang of steep ellipses, curving and carving, angled and making big waft as if a giant dog had coughed its last. The plane kept still while the village moved. We expected him to machine-gun us, to round out the display; we wouldn't have minded at first. If having him buzz our second-story windows meant we had to have a war, then we wanted War. He survived, with a chestful of ribbons fit to blind you, whereas the young bomber pharmacist from Tatlow's fragrant store across the road, the one with the Distinguished Flying Cross and the quiet manner, he had gone down into a German dam and would never be coming home. I later thought of how innocuous Plumtree's name was, how little like a warrior's. We expected something soft and pulpy to come from that, not this fondly remembered boomerang of scythes, the propeller in pain, the air ahead of it all bundled up and away with nowhere to go. I remembered best of all the engine, its careless abundant huge throb, taking us all after it into the airless azure where you lived and died in sheepskin. Years after, at the same rank as he had then, I was teaching geography to NCO aces, so they could become officers and gentlemen at zero feet.

DIANE ACKERMAN

She has serious hair, which I have always called her coal-black weather system, and often her face vanishes into it on a windy day as some stars into those coalsacks we find in the Milky Way. One of the finest poets alive, she rattles off wit as if she has rehearsed, saying as we buy an up-to-date guide to recorded music, "After many a summer dies the *Schwann*." It was almost a Proustian reference too. She loves the word *marcescent,* which means "withering without falling off." She applies it to her car, which she never bothers to fix, neither the door that won't close nor the dangling muffler nor the broken taillight. One day they will all get left behind. She has T. E. Lawrence's love of deserted places and believes, as I do not, in the hegemony of fact. She will always reign from a bath rich with essence of vanilla while slaves bring her camomile tea to set on the honed plank athwart the sides. My chore is to select a plastic bag and fit it smoothly around the inside of her bathroom's trash bin, a task she has borrowed for me from a character of mine, whose adventures began in the room next door. By her bed she has a framed enlargement of Jean

Marais in the role of the Beast from *La Belle et la Bête*. The word processor is her palace of delights, the kangaroo her favorite animal, the apricot her fruit. She ties the laces on her running shoes into big bows with enormous loops.

Summer nights, hemmed in during sleep by all that hair, she tumbles out of bed to wander and fidget while I sneak in there from my typewriter to hold her pillow against the grille of the air conditioner, whose tireless dry angelus makes the linen cool and fresh again.

P.W.

Some thwarted graffitist in a glossy magazine, a friend calls to tell me, has drawn a pyramid of fiction and who's who in it, as if we were all bricks, tapering amalgamated to the apex where the Nobel winners roost with ass-cracks crosswise on the razor blade of fame. One name, however, floats in the air around the pyramid, unattached to group or clique. Literally, there is no one to touch him, says my friend; he is out on his own and gaining altitude on his way to Orion. I wonder who drew this reassuring cone and thank him for putting my name where it can breathe.